and is punishable by up to 5 years in Federal prison and a fine of up to $250,000.

WARNING

THIS BOOK IS DARK. It's sexy, hot, and intense. The author is human, just as you are. Is the book perfect? It's as perfect as I could make it. Are there mistakes? Probably, then again, even New York Times top published books have minimal mistakes because, like me, they have human editors. There are words in this book that are not in the standard dictionary because they set the stage for a paranormal-urban fantasy world. Words in this novel are common in paranormal books and give better descriptions of the action in the story than other words found in standard dictionaries. They are intentional and not mistakes.

About the hero: chances are you may not fall instantly in love with him, that's because I don't write men you instantly love; you grow to love them. I don't believe in instant love. I write flawed, raw, caveman-like assholes that eventually let you see their redeeming qualities. They are aggressive assholes, one step above a caveman when we meet them. You may *not* even like him by the time you finish this book, but I promise you will love him by the end of this series.

About the heroine: There is a chance you might think she's naïve or weak, but then again, who starts out as a badass? Badass women are a product of growth, and I am going to put her through hell, and you get to watch her come up swinging every time I knock her on her ass. That's just how I do things. How she reacts to the set of circumstances she is put through may not be how you, as the reader, or I, as the author, would react to that same situation. Everyone reacts differently to circumstances and how she responds to her challenges is how I see her as a character and as a person.

I don't write love stories: I write fast-paced, knock you on your ass, *make you sit on the edge of your seat wondering what is going to happen next* in the books. If you're looking for cookie-cutter romance, this isn't for you. If you can't handle the ride, *unbuckle your seatbelt and get out of the roller-coaster car now.* If not, you've been warned. If nothing outlined above bothers you, carry on and enjoy the ride!

FYI, this is not a romance novel. They're going

to kick the shit out of each other, and if they
end up together, well, that's their choice. If you
are going into this blind, and you complain about
abuse between two creatures that are NOT human,
well, that's on you. I have done my job and given a
warning.

BOOKS BY AMELIA HUTCHINS ALONG WITH READING ORDER FOR SERIES

Books in bold lettering are unreleased

LEGACY OF THE NINE REALMS

Flames of Chaos

Ashes of Chaos

Ruins of Chaos

Crown of Chaos

Queen of Chaos

King of Chaos

Reign of Chaos

The Fae Chronicles

Fighting Destiny

Taunting Destiny

Escaping Destiny

Seducing Destiny

Unraveling Destiny

Embracing Destiny

Crowning Destiny

Finished Series

THE ELITE GUARDS

A Demon's Dark Embrace

Claiming the Dragon King

The Winter Court

A Demon's Plaything

A Touch of Fae

Wickedly Fae

A GUARDIAN'S DIARY

Darkest Before Dawn

Death before Dawn

Midnight Rising

MONSTERS SERIES

Playing with Monsters

Sleeping with Monsters
Becoming his Monster
Revealing the Monster
Finished Series

WICKED KNIGHTS

Oh, Holy Knight
If She's Wicked
If He's Wicked

MIDNIGHT COVEN BOOKS
Forever Immortal
Immortal Hexes
Midnight Coven
Finished Series

BULLETPROOF DAMSEL SERIES
Bulletproof Damsel
Silverproof Damsel
Fireproof Damsel

Alpha's Claim Standalone

Within the Darkness
Moon-Kissed

Night-Kissed

THE DARKEST FAE
King of the Shadow Fae
King of the Night Fae
Queen of the Stars

RED FLAGS
The Devil of London

FATED BY DESTINY
Whispers of Fate (Intro to Kahleena's book)

Witchery Hollows
A Discovery of Demonology
Into Neverland

SUPERNATURAL SYNDICATE
The Fixer
His to Control

If you're following the Fae Chronicles, Elite Guards, and Monsters series, the reading order is as follows.

Fighting Destiny
Taunting Destiny

Escaping Destiny

Seducing Destiny

A Demon's Dark Embrace

Playing with Monsters

Unraveling Destiny

Sleeping with Monsters

Claiming the Dragon King

Oh, Holy Knight

Becoming his Monster

A Demon's Plaything

The Winter Court

If She's Wicked

Embracing Destiny

Crowning Destiny

Revealing the Monster

Whispers of Fate

CHAPTER ONE

MOIRA

JOHN DENVER'S "COUNTRY ROAD" hummed through the rental car's speakers, and I belted out the lyrics as I turned off the highway and onto the long, winding road leading over the mountains. I'd left home at seventeen to study abroad in Ireland five years ago. My last visit home had been after I'd finished my bachelor's degree before heading off to Boston to attend Harvard, but it hadn't been nearly long enough of a visit. Plus, my grandmother had been busy with orders for the apothecary shop, then the yearly celebrations Witchery Hollow held at the end of summer. When all that was over, I'd spirited off across the country to attend classes on herbology, alchemy and pretty much anything which kept my mind occupied. Of course, I'd thought there would be time to tell grandmother, the woman who'd raised me, all about my endless adventures. Instead, I'd received a brief message that had stopped me dead in my tracks.

The woman who'd taken me in as an infant was dying.

Moments after I'd received the message, I'd quit both jobs I'd been working to pay off the endless student debt I'd accrued in Ireland. Next, I'd phoned my professors and explained I wouldn't be able to attend classes anymore, or help them correct the endless piles of tests they'd allowed to stack up. After I'd finished quitting my jobs and dropping out of school, I'd packed my entire apartment in Boston into a rental car and started toward the one place I'd ever considered home. Witchery Hollow.

Witchery Hollow was a picturesque town in the middle of the Selkirk Mountains. In fact, it would never be found on a map. The flourishing green forests of the Idaho Panhandle were serene and mostly uninhabited. Of course, the terrain was rocky until you passed through the valley, which then changed to lush, rolling hills of greenery. In short, there weren't many visitors to our tiny mountaintop town. It was how the locals preferred it, or at least the older ones.

The lack of people was why my mother, Rena Bishop, had left at the first chance she'd gotten. She'd gone off to Harvard and graduated with full honors, which was a stark contrast to my barely passing grades. I'd been working several jobs to pay off the debt I'd picked up at the first college. I'd also been pursuing multiple classes outside of Harvard as well, to finish the secondary degrees I'd chosen to pursue. After she'd left Harvard, she'd joined Doctors

Without Borders. While on vacation, she'd had a hot and heavy relationship with one of her married colleagues in Italy, before ending it to move on to her next adventure. Unfortunately, the result of her whirlwind romance was me.

My mother had returned to Witchery Hollow only long enough to leave me with my grandmother before heading back to work. Then she'd gone and died before I could ask her why she'd chosen to leave me behind. The knowledge of who my father was had died with her.

The song playing became ear-splitting static, which had me leaning forward to scan through the stations for another. After a moment with no success in finding a signal, I groaned and glanced up, just as I flew by a sign indicating a sharp turn up ahead. Placing both hands back on the steering wheel, I navigated the curve and then turned my attention back to the radio, trying to get it to connect to my Bluetooth.

The next time I glanced back at the road, which wasn't more than a second later, a cry of horror escaped my lips and my foot slammed on the brake pedal, but I was too late to avoid my front bumper slamming into an animal. The loud *screech* of metal buckling filled the cab. The squealing of the tires tore through the car as the back end began fishtailing over the pavement. When the car finally came to a stop, it was in a ditch with the ass-end pointed up at the night sky.

"Shit, shit, shit!" I screamed while slamming my hands on the wheel. "This is why I can't have nice things!"

The rebel in me hated listening to reason. I learned nothing the easy way, ever. Peering over my shoulder, I grumbled. It wasn't like I could sit here, either. In a ditch. In the dark. Alone.

"Don't do it, Moira. Do not be the woman who gets eaten by wildlife because she's too stupid to stay in the car. No. Nope. Not happening." I exhaled a shuddered puff of air before groaning. "But if you don't check on the poor thing, you'll spend the entire night wondering if you're a murderer. Why am I like this?"

With the decision made, which was a stupid-ass decision, I opened the door and slowly climbed out. My heels sank into the wet soil, which led to an unimpressed mutter escaping from my lips. After climbing up the bank of the ditch, I paused long enough to take in the awkward angle of the car, noting that it would be nearly impossible to get out without help from a tow truck, and then I frowned at the dark object on the roadway.

"Add 'murderer of poor wildlife' to my pathetic resume," I muttered, uncertain if the animal was alive or dead. "Did you die?" My voice echoed through the valley, which caused me to jump in surprise. "You're such a badass, Moira." After berating my own foolish, overactive imagination, I crept forward. The large dog-like animal lifted its head at my approach, and it let out a rumble of unfriendly sounds, seemingly warning me to stay back, and I froze in place.

"Easy boy—or girl . . . whichever you are. I'm not here to hurt you. I mean, I totally hit you and am guilty of removing my eyes from the roadway, but I didn't mean to do it." Taking a few calming breaths, I snorted at my own foolishness. "Look, it wasn't my fault the radio was static, which, let's be honest here, isn't something any person *or* animal enjoys listening to. Am I right? I can't be expected to listen to it for the rest of the drive home. Yes, I definitely should've waited until I'd rounded the turn, but we can't all be perfect!"

The large canine watched me with amber eyes, as if it were judging my stupidity more than I was. "Can you walk or move? I'd hate for you to get run over and be flattened on the road. It wouldn't be good luck, bud." When the canine just continued baring his teeth, I puffed out a frustrated breath. "Now I'm talking to animals in the middle of nowhere in the dark. See? This is why they call women crazy. You don't look like you want my help, but here my dumbass is, trying to save you." Moving toward the center of the road, I scanned the creature's side for any sign of damage. "Up, let's go." The animal slowly rose to its feet, baring sharp, pointy teeth as it did so. "Shoo, Cujo.

Hit the road, Jack . . . Oh, that might be a sore subject still. You know, with me hitting you?" The huge canine growled menacingly.

"Oh, God! Don't eat me," I pleaded, as it began prowling forward. "Listen, I don't taste good. I wouldn't even taste good with ranch or ketchup lathered over me. I'm the kind of taste you won't be able to get out of those surprisingly long teeth you have. Great, now I'm Little Red Riding Hood, damn it. How did I know I'd regret getting out of the car? Good doggy? No!" I cried as it snapped its teeth and tried to take a bite out of me.

Dancing out of the limping, angry canine's bite radius, I held up my hands as if that would placate the guy. "If you eat me, you'll feel like a serious asshole when you figure out that I was only trying to help you! You don't eat the helping hand. It's like a rule or some shit, right? Shit—"

The echo of a fast-moving vehicle met my eardrums as my eyes lifted from the animal to the direction I'd come from, just as the car rounded the bend. Blinded by the headlights, I lifted my arms as if it would stop the vehicle which was barreling toward me from actually colliding with me.

A scream tore free from my lungs as fur brushed against my leg and the animal abandoned me to my fate. I didn't even have time to laugh at the irony of being in the spot or position of the animal when I'd hit it, before the screeching of brakes tore through the night. *Karma sucked!*

My arms remained over my face as I silently prayed for the pearly gates to open and admit me before the pain of being hit by a car set in. The ding of a door opening was followed immediately by the rich, masculine rage of the person who almost punched my ticket. My hands slowly began patting over my body as I trembled so hard my teeth ached from it.

"Are you trying to fucking die?" An angry, sharp tone clapped through the silent night. "What are you doing standing in the middle of the fucking road at this ungodly hour?" the irate driver demanded in a smooth, dark timbre, causing goosebumps to spread over every inch of me. "I asked you a question, lady!"

A hand landed on my shoulder, yanking me around. It forced fear to jolt through me as I peered up at the man. His headlights cut through the darkness around us. They also were making it impossible to see him beyond the shadows obscuring his features from sight.

"I'm sorry," I whispered past my trembling lips. "I hit an animal and then stopped to see if it needed help."

"And you thought it wise to stand in the middle of the road and do what, join it as roadkill? Brilliant, lady."

"I'm aware of that fact, sir," I spit out crossly at his angered response.

He shifted his posture, which caused his headlights to blind me once more. Shielding my eyes from the light with my arm, I opened my mouth to explain more, but only a whisper of shock came out. I was rendered speechless by the man, who was currently examining me in return.

The moment he stepped closer, I was given an even closer view of the darkly tantalizing specimen of man before me. His nearness caused everything around me to go silent, as if the entire world died instead of me on the highway.

Dark, silky-smooth hair framed an arrogant face. A proud nose sat between finely chiseled cheekbones, which whispered of aristocratic lineage. The dusting of a five o'clock shadow kissed his jawline, and his full, lush lips promised to deliver every filthy fantasy I'd ever held in my dreams. He was taller than me by a good foot, and he wore a crisp, clean dress shirt that did little to conceal the sinewy muscles hidden beneath the thin fabric. The shirt was unbuttoned at the collar revealing ink beneath it. More was revealed from the sleeves rolled up on his forearms to expose dark, sexy ink that began on both wrists.

"Where's your car at?" he demanded as he scanned the dark highway, eyeing the barely visible trunk of my rented car.

Giving myself a mental shake, I berated myself for eyeing him like candy. I'd never been rendered speechless by anything, let alone by some man.

The ominous feeling of being watched jerked my attention to his vehicle, which had men leaning against it, observing us. The light made it impossible to judge anything about them since they were obscured by the darkness. Obviously, I'd been very distracted as I'd ogled the guy.

Biting my lip between my teeth nervously, I returned my focus to the man nearest to me. Stepping to the side to get out of the headlights' blinding glare, I silently calculated my chances of reaching my car before he could prevent me from locking myself inside of it, to call for help. Zilch. Considering the length of his legs compared to mine, I'd make it maybe five steps before he'd catch me. If his intention wasn't to kidnap me, I'd look like a foolish girl who'd locked herself in her *very* stuck car.

I was regretting not informing my grandmother of my plans to return home. No one would even realize I'd gone missing except my grandmother, which would have the local authorities calling my job, which I'd quit, or the college, which I'd dropped out of. In short, I was screwed if this guy and his buddies were of a mind to make me disappear.

The idea of being discarded in a ditch wasn't appealing.

Plus, I'd probably end up chewed on by the animal I'd hit and stopped to check on. Wouldn't that shit be ironic? Talk about the circle of life, Moira. Congratulations, you're a freaking idiot sandwich!

Smoldering, gray eyes slid back to clash with mine, while I watched his features darkening in the moonlight. His demeanor changed the moment our eyes locked, as if he'd discovered something he didn't like about me. The way they roved over my face before gradually drifting down my frame with a look of disdain, sent some uncertainty through me. What had shifted to place the look on his face?

"Bishop, I take it," he said in a way that made me think he found the name foul on his tongue.

"And you are?" I countered in a saccharine tone.

"Done here," he growled, turning to leave.

Placing my hands on my hips, I simmered with the arrogance of the smug prick. "Good riddance, asshole," I muttered beneath my breath, stiffening as he paused as the words left my lips.

Staring at my car stuck in the ditch, I frowned. There was no way I could get the car out without help, not with the front end sunk into the damp earth. I'd been lucky the airbags hadn't deployed. The man leaned against the trunk, smirking seconds before the thunderous clang of them deploying tore through the silent night. I gasped as glass peppered the ground. "Son of a bitch!" I snapped as hopelessness drifted through me.

"I believe the words you are looking for are 'thank you'," He stated icily as he removed invisible lint from his shirt before returning his heavy gaze toward me. "Next time, stay on the road, woman. He wasn't worth your life, was he? No, so I'd suggest you think before you act so foolishly. Were you distracted, or just not thinking about your own safety?" Parting my lips to argue his words, I closed them as dark shadows fell over us from his men moving closer to stand at the edge of the roadway. Peering toward the men, who were slowly moving toward the mess I'd made of the rental, I felt a prickle of fear and apprehension slivering through my flesh. "Answer the question, Bishop."

Anger bristled through me at the audacity of this guy. Was he pissed because I'd placed the animal's safety over my own? Why was it endearing, yet irritating? Fisting my hands at my sides, I felt the exhaustion and pushing myself to continue on this late at night colliding together. At the innocent tilt of his head while scanning my face, I felt my blood boiling. Choosing violence, my shoulders straightened as I gritted my teeth.

"My name isn't *Bishop*," I shot back irritably. "And I was *thinking* I didn't want to leave the poor thing to suffer in the middle of the road!"

Dismissing him outright, I began to descend the incline sideways to avoid landing in a heap at the bottom. The dress I'd thrown on this morning wasn't ideal for trekking through undergrowth, but I did my best not to scratch up my legs as I made my way down the slope. At the bottom, I sent a silent prayer heavenward that I'd made it down gracefully.

I huffed at the sight of broken glass from the airbags deploying. The interior was covered in a white, powdery substance, which also dusted my bags in the passenger seat. Opening the door, I bent forward to retrieve my purse, but a hand gripped my bicep, yanking me back as the car door was slammed closed.

"What the hell do you think you're doing? Unhand me, now!" I ordered in a sharp, frigid tone. "Remove your hand from me, sir."

"I don't think so, Bishop." The look of disdain I'd glimpsed earlier had changed into intrigue. "I'm aware of every Bishop witch in Witchery Hollow. So, how is it I don't know you?"

"I'm sorry, but what?" I demanded with silent laughter bubbling up from my chest. "Did you just insult me by calling me a witch or are you insane?" I was leaning toward both, really.

He was entirely too hot not to be majorly flawed in some way or another. But he'd literally just attached the

Bishop name to *witches*. As if this night wasn't strange enough already? Of course, he could be superstitious as some who dwelled within Witchery Hollow were. Hell, I'd chosen to attend Harvard because of its proximity to Salem, and the link my family had to the famous witch trials.

Salem was merely an hour-long drive away from Boston if you left before traffic picked up. I'd spent endless days of exploring the city, or digging up anything I could find on Bridget Bishop. She'd been the first woman to be accused of witchcraft. She also happened to be my ancestor. Maybe he thought himself some sort of puritan? Another red flag to add to the growing list of them.

His incredulous eyes scanned my face before he turned, peering over his shoulder at the men standing silently behind us on the road. A dark, wickedly-sinful laugh escaped his throat as he returned his soul-stealing gaze back to where I watched him. The hold he had on my arm tightened as he forced me backward, and I gasped as my back pressed against the solid surface of my car. Swallowing the fear his presence created, I refused to cower or beg him to release me.

"If you are a Bishop, it would make Violet your grandmother," he demanded in a curious tone laced with lust, as his eyes slowly dipped to the curvature of my breasts exposed by the deep V-line of my bodice. His

13

fingers pinched the strands of my icy-blonde hair as if he were testing the texture of it before drawing it to his nose, inhaling deeply. Those unsettling eyes held mine prisoner as he released it, even as his lips twisted into a dangerous smile.

"Definitely a Bishop. I don't remember hearing about any of Violet's daughters being bred other than Scarlett." He turned to look toward the men lingering on the roadway. "Do you guys remember hearing about the other two procreating?" When they just laughed, his focus returned to me. "I'm very aware of all of Scarlett's daughters and where they currently are. So, which Bishop bitch do you belong to?"

"Do you honestly expect me to respond to that? *Bred*? Who the hell says shit like that? And if you knew every Bishop, you'd know Rena had a child, too."

I wasn't some secret lovechild. Okay, so technically I *was*, but not from the people in town. It didn't hurt for this asshole to know who my mother was. I attempted to duck beneath his arm to escape the electrical current his proximity caused against my skin. One of his hands landed on my hip as the other gripped my chin to jerk my face up until I teetered on my tiptoes. Panic and anger combined into a dangerous combination as he manhandled me.

"Rena is your mother?"

Ignoring his question, I shot off one of my own. "What do you want from me?" I fumed through clenched teeth.

"I want your name, darling," he answered smoothly.

Blinking slowly, I chewed over which name I should offer the smug prick. Did it really matter if I told him the truth? No. It might also get him to leave me alone since our family was one of the original settlers here, which carried some sway.

"Moira Bishop," I admitted, and he leaned closer with his nostrils flaring. The sound of his teeth grinding caused my hackles to rise because, clearly, he detested my last name for some reason.

"Moira Bishop," he whispered as if he was tasting it on his devilish tongue. "How is it that they managed to keep you hidden for this long? A pretty thing like you, well, you'd be a hard thing to keep hidden."

"I'm not sure if that's intended as an insult or compliment."

A shiver rushed through me as he pushed my head to the side before running his nose over the delicate line of my collarbone. Unhurriedly, methodically, he drifted it against my flesh until the warmth of his breath wafted against my earlobe. Pressure built in my abdomen as my thighs pressed together and I tried to ignore the pulse he'd created between them.

His proximity caused my nipples to pebble until they

strained against the bodice of my dress. His thumb ran along the line of my jaw, and I hated the whimper of sound escaping my lips as much as his soft laughter tickling my ear.

"Take it however you like, Bishop. I don't care how you interpret what I say," he growled before nipping at my jaw, which elicited a visceral response from my body.

My hands lifted to press against his chest but didn't go farther than feeling the sinewy muscles beneath the thin dress shirt. The way he pressed his body harder against me had my lips parting as a soft exhale left my lungs. "You don't have the normal Bishop coloring," he pointed out.

"Why is that?"

"How would I know?" I murmured weakly.

Giving in to the exhaustion, I rested my head against the car before I ended up with a kink in my neck. He allowed it, but his heated lips took it as an invitation. They skimmed over my throat before moving to hover a breath away from mine.

"That's something you should be asking my mother, not me."

"Admittedly, I think I prefer your pretty emerald-green eyes to the Bishops' cold, dreary blue ones." Straightening, he towered over me. The hand left my throat to brace his weight against the car, even as the one on my hip gripped hard enough to force a hiss from my lips. My palms caressed over the solid muscles of his chest absently, even as I frowned. "You're in quite the quandary. Aren't you?"

"Am I?" I whispered through the heaviness of my tongue. What the hell was wrong with me? I'd never responded to any man in this manner.

"Aren't you?" his dark, whiskey smooth tone had my insides melting.

"You're in my personal space." There, I'd at least made it known I had boundaries.

"Is that so?" he asked before pressing against me until I couldn't discern my damn name.

"Yes, you are." The breathy whisper of sound escaped as a moan.

"I'm going to guess no one knows you're returning home tonight. Do they?"

At my audible swallow, his smile turned wolfish. Blood was heating my face as arousal rushed to my pussy. There was something animalistic in the way he stared at me.

His presence was primal, despotic, and predacious. As if he could bend me over the hood, and I'd be the one pleading for him to devour me whole.

"No, I didn't think so. Violet wouldn't have been able to keep it a secret from me. So, your car is stuck in a ditch and there's no cell reception in this valley. It's rather troublesome. Isn't it?"

"I have two feet and enough stubbornness to endure the long walk to Witchery Hollow alone." It wasn't a bluff, per se. I was full of tenacity, and I did, in fact, have two feet. But walking the rest of the way home would be hellish.

"I bet you're stubborn enough to attempt walking it, too." Those hauntingly beautiful eyes scanned my face before snorting. "It's a very long walk in those dainty shoes, Bishop."

"You're heading in that direction. Aren't you?" I countered as his hand left my hip to place his palm on my cheek.

"Indeed, I am. Ask me for a ride," he murmured as he stepped back from pressing against me, but not far enough to allow me to pass. The wolfish smile on his mouth warned me of what his answer would be.

I snorted loudly. "Why? So, you can say no? A gentleman would've offered a ride. They wouldn't demand a lady ask or beg him for one." I shoved him away as the realization that I'd been fondling his magnificent chest sank in to my lust-drunk brain. "No thank you, whatever-your-name-is."

"I never claimed to be a gentleman. Did I? Because I assure you, it would be a preposterous lie."

"No, I guess you didn't. But men like you, you're better off as enemies than anything else, sir," I muttered, pegging him with a withering stare.

"You don't want to make me your enemy. You wouldn't survive me. I wouldn't grant you any mercy, darling."

Again, I opened the car door and grabbed my purse before blindly digging through it for my phone. I swiped over the screen, glared at the *No Service* message where the bars should have been, and then turned a withering expression on him.

My effort was wasted since he was too busy staring at my bare thighs, and when I pointedly cleared my throat, he slowly dragged his gaze up to my face.

"When you get home, do tell Violet that I'll be over for tea at noon. Make sure she bakes scones and brews the proper tea for a guest of my . . . *standing*. I'm certain she'll be delighted you and I have been properly introduced without her privy for our introductions."

Because that wasn't ominous as shit?

"How am I supposed to tell her who is coming to tea if I don't know your name?"

Was this asshole serious? I felt like I'd fallen into some movie where everyone else was in the know, but I was left in the dark.

Tossing my phone on the seat of the car, I leaned in further, grabbing out the soft ballet flats I'd had in the seat, kicking off one heel to slide one on, then the other. There was no way I was climbing the ditch in heels again. My thighs were already screaming from the first time and then side-stepping down the damn thing.

"Rowan Teivel. Tell Violet that I'm looking forward to having tea with *both* of you." His smile was roguish and filled with amusement, as if he found something hilarious.

"I take it she doesn't care for you much?"

"I assume there's no man in your life?" His eyes slid over my body with naked hunger before rolling back up to my face.

"That's a personal question. You and I aren't going to do personal questions on a dark road in the moonlight, Teivel," I returned in an acrimoniously sharp tone. "Have a delightful night, and thank you for not hitting me. I'd say it's been a pleasure, but it would be a blatant lie." When I bent to snatch up my phone, purse and shoes, I felt his eyes on me.

Huffing with irritation, I straightened and slammed the door closed, before once again, climbing from the ditch. I winced repeatedly as the sharp rocks bit painfully into my feet through the thin slippers, but I eventually made it to the trunk and managed to open it so I could grab my backpack and shove random items I'd need for the night into it.

"And I don't see any men here, so asking about any would be a moot point and waste of air." I dropped my purse in the trunk so I could dig through another bag for my Vans slip-on tennis shoes. Kicking off the ballet flats,

I winced at the gravel against the soles of my feet. Once I had them on my poor feet, I went to grab my purse out of the trunk, only for him to snatch it before I could. "Give me my purse, now," I demanded as the reins on my mood snapped.

"Stop being childish and ask me for a ride, Moira Darling."

"How did you know my middle name was Darling?"

His eyes widened, and a blinding smile spread over his lips. "I didn't, but I can't say I'm shocked that Rena named you Moira *Darling* Bishop. That girl always had an unhealthy obsession with Peter Pan."

I'd been wrong. His eyes weren't merely gray. They were the color of freshly pressed steel with a dark line of blue surrounding the iris.

"Get in my car. It's late, and there are ravenous beasts prowling these woods. And you? You look fucking delicious enough to eat."

Swallowing past the uneasiness flooding my mind, I chanced a peek at the men silently watching us with curious gazes.

"They won't bite unless I give them permission to do so. It's me you should be worried about." The way his smile turned wolfish even as his eyes glimmered with something dangerous dancing in their steel-colored depths, wasn't encouraging.

CHAPTER TWO

MOIRA

THE RIDE UP THE mountain was filled with tension. Rowan had instructed the men with him to pile into the back and then turned music on, ending any chance of conversation. I didn't mind, but I was curious to know how he assumed my mother had been obsessed with Peter Pan. In actuality, she'd named me Grimoira Darling Bishop, and Grandmother had shortened it because she'd thought it was absurd to name a child Grimoira.

I'd known every soul who called Witchery Hollow home, but I had no memory of Rowan or his cohorts. In fact, our family was one of the original families to call this place home. There wasn't anyone who didn't show grandmother the respect she deserved for being descended from the original settlers.

Fidgeting, I rubbed the ruffles at the hem of my dress between my thumb and forefinger while peering out into the passing countryside. The volume of the music lowered, and I turned toward Rowan and waited for what he wanted to say.

Rowan didn't speak, which left me floundering for something to say in order to fill the awkward silence. "When did you move to Witchery Hollow?" I asked. His lips jerked at the corners of his full, kissable mouth.

"You're assuming I've not always lived here?" he shot back as one dark brow lifted with his question.

"I'd know it if you'd lived here, Teivel. The town isn't big enough to hide in." It was probably large enough to hide in, but not for someone as handsome as Rowan. I'd have noticed he was here. My vagina would've definitely taken notice of his sex appeal.

"Where have you been for the last couple of years?" he asked.

Abandoning the soft taffeta skirt, I shifted in my seat, silently taking in the way his presence dominated the cab of the Land Rover. Normally, I'd be secretly checking out the details and gadgets of his expensive car, but I couldn't think beyond his presence. Licking my lips, I noted Rowan's eyes abandoning the road to zero-in on my mouth, then drifting up from them as a blush spread over my cheeks.

"I attended Trinity College for a few years, then returned to the States to take more classes at Harvard," I admitted, seeing no reason not to do so. The skin around his eyes tightened before he focused back on the road.

"What did you study?" he continued questioning.

"Herbology, homeopathic medicine, botanical medicine and alchemy, as well as things connected to those studies. Pseudoscience has always fascinated me, but alchemy is something I really love learning about." Someone in the backseat whistled, which caused Rowan to glance in the rearview mirror before settling his attention back on the road.

"You actually went to college even though you are a Bishop?"

"My mother went to college too. I fail to see why being a Bishop would prevent me from reaching for higher education. If anything, we should consider it an accomplishment since few from Witchery Hollow ever leave it, and those who do, rarely do so to better themselves." I felt as if he'd laughed at the accomplishments I'd achieved. "Do you think a woman cannot be educated?" My inner-feminist was rising at the way he'd asked.

"I know many well-educated women. I also know that when Bishop women wander too far from home and leave the protection of Witchery Hollow, they die young, like Rena did on her trek around the world," he stated softly, while gauging my response at his mention of my mother. If I had known her, I'd probably respond to her name. But I'd never met her and only knew her through the pictures and tales my grandmother told me. "I'm finding it hard to believe that Violet Bishop allowed you to leave, since you're rather young and naïve."

"That's quite the assumption since you've no idea how old I am," I retorted.

Briefly, his eyes abandoned the road to drift over my features slowly, dipping to my chest before they returned to the road. Even though he'd merely looked at me, it felt as if he'd dissected more than just my appearance.

"Twenty-four, or very close to it," he guessed, which had goosebumps spreading over my arms. "How old do you think I am, darling?"

"Thirty?" I blurted out the first guess that came to mind, which had laughter erupting from the backseat. "Late twenties?"

"She's cute, Rowan. Can we keep her? I bet she'd be fun to play with," one man asked. "I like new toys, even if I do end up breaking them."

"She's a Bishop. Which means she's more trouble than she's worth. Pussy isn't good enough for the shit you'd have to deal with to hit-it-and-quit-it, boys," another stated in a deadened tone. "Besides, Bishop women snare men with their vibrant red hair, and enthralling blue stare promising them their souls for eternity. Then, they devour your soul until nothing remains of who you were before the hag caught you in her pussy trap. You're smarter than that, dumbass. We don't play with them until they break. Everyone knows broken toys are no fun to play with."

"My hair isn't red, nor are my eyes blue. Besides, I wouldn't let any of you *play* with me even if I were desperate enough to ride my teddy bear until I got myself off," I returned with honey lathering in my reply. "But please, continue talking shit while I try to catch a fuck to give you, little boy." The moment the words slipped free, there was what sounded like a scuffle behind me, and a shiver of fear rushed down my spine. Still, I refused to turn to see what was happening.

"Enough," Rowan warned before turning the music back up and drowning out whatever sounds might come from the backseat.

Once the song ended, Boy Epic's "Dirty Mind" began filtering through the speakers.

The sultry undertones caused my stomach to clench with need twisting through it sharply. Sinful scenes began playing wickedly within my mind. My body came alive with a ravenous need to be played like guitar strings, thrummed with long, slender fingers until it sang another kind of tune. Unlike when I read or slept, the star of them wasn't faceless. It was Rowan, and that had my cheeks burning with embarrassment.

Watching him from beneath my lashes, I noted how his hands tightened on the steering wheel. Heat spread to my chest as his steel-colored eyes lowered to my thighs, as if he could sense my traitorous body responding to my overactive imagination. Turning away from him before he noticed the heat searing my face, I squeezed my eyes closed, barely containing a groan of humiliation as my nipples pushed against the bodice of my dress.

"Cold?" There was a taunting tenor to the question, which was followed by masculine amusement in the back seat.

"A little," I lied. It only made his smile grow more mischievous. Reaching behind him, he pulled a jacket off of the back of his seat before tossing it into my lap. "Thank you."

I hadn't expected him to give me his suit jacket, but I'd left my cardigan in the backseat of the rental car. As I slid it on, the scents of sage, bergamot, vetiver and the perfect amount of blackcurrant overtook my senses. The mixture was intoxicating. My lips parted as the propinquity to the scent warred against my senses. It disarmed me, leaving me drifting through an endless wave of lust as wetness built between my thighs.

A visible shiver rushed through me as the inebriating combination took control of my lust. It only took a single glance at Rowan to know he'd been aware of how I'd respond to the concoction of scents he'd knowingly wielded against me. The proof was there, shimmering in his eyes as he bit into his bottom lip. If I hadn't known better, I would have said he dabbled in alchemy himself.

I was an idiot for not catching the undertones of vetiver mixed with bergamot earlier. Sure, I'd smelled his masculine fragrance when he'd been pressed against me, but my brain had been bombarded with what was happening, then dismissed it easily when his presence overshadowed everything else.

He'd short-circuited my brain and overwhelmed me until I'd been rendered a brain-dead idiot by the intensity of his overwhelming charisma.

"Something wrong, Bishop?"

Wrong? Yes, there were a number of things wrong, but the biggest was that the aphrodisiac was strong enough to have my pussy soaked with anticipation.

It pissed me off to no end since I couldn't get off tonight. My personal collection of toys was in the car I'd left behind. I blamed that for my temporary moment of lunacy.

"Not at all." If the fucker wanted to play? I'd step up to the board.

Uncurling my fingers, I slowly gripped the hem of my skirt, then leisurely pulled it up to the crest of my thighs so he could see the soft-pink lace of my panties. Parting my legs, I ran my fingertips over the inside of my thighs. Purposely running them higher on my legs, I pushed my fingertips into my panties and then slid them over my freshly-waxed pussy. Pleasure burst through me at the fainted touch of my fingers against my sex. Worrying my lip with my teeth, a needy whimper vibrated my throat before escaping as a husky moan.

A horn blared, causing Rowan to jerk the car back into the correct lane to avoid a head-on collision, and I gave him an innocent smile.

"Something wrong, Rowan?" I asked in a saccharine voice filled with mock worry.

"Careful, Bishop. You bait the beast, you might bite off more than you're willing to chew," he warned in a raspy tone of pure, brutal lust.

Heat curled in my belly as my sex clenched, uncaring of propriety or decency. What the hell was happening to me? I wasn't this brazen, emboldened nymphomaniac. Sure, I liked having filthy sex and never allowed the world to judge me for my more sinister kinks.

It was the age of monster smut, after all, and immoral desires were in these days. Sex was no longer held to the high standards of society's decree or wedlock. It wasn't just between a man and a woman. Shit, I'd been the center of an orgy a time or two, and hadn't given two filthy shits if someone snapped a few dirty pictures while I'd been in the throes of coming and had hands fondling and petting every sinful inch of me.

"Don't assume you know what I can handle, Teivel," I shot back, and his nostrils flared as if he could smell my state of arousal. "I'm a grown-ass woman, one who isn't afraid of her overcharged libido or sexuality." Smiling at the hooded look on his darkening face, I turned to stare back out at the moonlit countryside. "But I am impressed by the fact that you mixed vetiver with bergamot. From the balance of their scents, it's clear you were aware of it becoming an aphrodisiac but mindful enough not to end up smelling like cat piss. Most people learn of its unique properties and overuse it, which does the exact opposite of what they intended it to do."

"Your grandmother sells only the best tonics and elixirs in her shop. If she didn't, she'd be dead by now." Whipping my head toward his smug, arrogant face, I glowered.

"Are you threatening my grandmother?" The men snickered behind me.

"I don't threaten anyone. If they piss me off, I simply handle them accordingly. Unfortunately, the Bishop bloodline has had immunity from me because they have something I want, but I'll get it eventually, one way or another."

"And what is it you want?" I asked, barely concealing my curiosity.

"Something that was stolen from me a very long time

ago. I intend to get it back, and if I don't, the consequences will be disastrous for everyone involved."

Blinking slowly, I tried not to get annoyed by his ambiguous answer. Still, the meaning was clear enough. "It sounds like a threat, *darling*."

I'd added a sultry tone as he turned onto the road leading toward Witchery Hollow. Moments later, we pulled up to the impressive gate blocking a gated neighborhood. At the far end of the long driveway beyond the gate, there was a mansion with immense columns and a wraparound porch. If I squinted, I could make out several men decked-out in black fatigues standing sentry.

"Get out," he snapped, and when I reached for the door handle, he grabbed my bicep. "Not you, Bishop. The rest of you, go. Moira and I are going to have a conversation before I drop her off. I'll return once we've concluded our talk." The men snickered before exiting the car and moving to the gate before it swung open, allowing Rowan to drive through.

The car shot forward, but Rowan's expression turned dark as his body tensed. He was staying at the Gowdie Estate? I'd often snuck onto the estate to pilfer herbs from the extensive, overgrown gardens. It was less than a mile from the Bishop Estate, which bordered the land of several of the older, more prominent families living in Witchery Hollow. Not that all of us were in the same mountain range. Some had distanced themselves from others over time while some left Witchery Hollow altogether.

"You're staying at the Gowdie Estate?" I asked softly as he passed the road that would lead to grandmother's gated drive. "You missed the driveway for my house."

Rowan turned down the old creek road and slowed to a crawl before he turned to face me. "I'm aware. Get out of the car," he demanded.

My heartbeat thumped against my ribcage so hard I was convinced it would bruise. Fear shot through me as he put the vehicle in park, even as I floundered for what to do. My lips parted to speak, but the door was yanked open, and I was pulled from the car before I realized he'd even exited the vehicle. A startled cry left my lips as he pushed me against the door and palmed my throat, forcing me to look up at him.

"I don't like being fucked with," he growled while his darkening gaze plunged to my lips.

"I'm not the asshole who started it, am I?" I demanded as my chest heaved with anticipation and fear roiling through me.

What the hell was I doing? There was nothing I wanted more right at this moment, then to be bent over the hood of his car, and railed until I howled at the moon like a bitch in heat.

"What's the matter, Rowan? Don't like it when a

woman plays a man's game?" I was taunting him, which he didn't like if the tightening of his hand against my throat was anything to go off of.

My eyes grew heavily hooded at the silent threat and power he held with it there. I was playing with fire, and praying to get burned by it.

"Yeah, most men don't seem to like it when the bitch fights back. And I do, and I play dirty because I'm not ashamed of being filthy."

"Is that so?" His voice was a rumble of sound that scraped over my nipples before twisting around my clit.

If sex had a voice, it would be whispered words in the same primal, masculine noise he'd just made. Wickedly dark promises of filthy intentions that would devour you as it railed your naked body into a pile of sated bliss.

"Be honest with me, Bishop. Would you let me bend your lithe body over the hood, then fuck your needy cunt while those titties are cleaning the bug guts from my grill?"

Talk about a mood killer! Rowan had destroyed my fantasy at the mention of bugs. But he'd driven the nail home in the coffin at *guts*. Swallowing down the bravado, I snorted.

"You're not some backwoods country slut who'd want that sort of shit. You're more of a flower in the meadow, with the moonlight bathing your naked flesh in its pale light. And damn, you'd be so pretty with that light, shimmering hair fanning out beneath you as your legs are draped over my shoulders, as I'm feasting gluttonously on your wet, pink cunt." His eyes sparkled with amusement as the air escaped my lungs on a whisper of sound. "Don't worry, I'd be certain to fuck your body ruthlessly into the dirt until we were both filthy and covered in mud from sweating while we rutted like wild animals beneath the moon."

"I . . . You're . . . very . . ." Words failed to come to mind with the way my body erupted with affirmation that he'd pegged me correctly. I wanted filthy, deplorable sex. Absolutely, but I was also a lady who wanted some romance tossed in, no matter how haphazardly it was added.

"Don't like it when a man isn't afraid to call you out on your shit? I promise you, I'm man enough to call your bluff, darling. You like baiting men, but you're not willing to give up your worth for a quick fuck. I commend you for it, but I'm entitled to be enraged and hate myself for not being low enough to take what you're offering me. The thought of fucking your naked, wet cunt and getting off is so bloody tempting. But then you'd pull up those pretty pink panties and fuck off into that mansion of yours. My come would trickle down your thighs like a cold reminder of how I'd used your body like some easy pussy, and you'd fucking hate me before you ever reached the shower. Because that's how shit works out when lust consumes humans and they act like animals. You don't even know if I actually want you, or if I am merely interested in the easy pussy at hand."

My hand moved before my brain registered what he'd stated. The loud sound of my palm colliding against his cheek was startling in the eerily silent night. His hold on my throat tightened as he slowly turned back with murderous rage simmering in his mercury-colored depths.

His hand tightened on my throat before I was jerked forward toward his body, before then being forced back against the side of the car.

"Please don't kill me. I'm not even thirty yet! Honestly, my life's been really unremarkable and I haven't even gotten to the good part yet. Plus. . ." I lost the ability to think coherently as his erection pressed against my ass. "That's a dick." That was a fucking *dick!* It was huge, and thick as it weighed into my spine.

My breathing became labored as arousal flooded my core, begging for me to take on the challenge he was offering with the monstrous weapon concealed in his slacks.

"Are you certain about that?" His silky whisper sent his breath fanning the nape of my neck. "Is this what you were imagining as you touched yourself? Were you imagining that it was me touching you instead of your fingers?"

Aww, he thought my cunt was pretty? He had a sweet side! Or maybe I was insane? Had I actually died on the highway and this was heaven? I wasn't complaining to management if that was the case.

"What's the matter? Your familiar got that pink tongue tied up, darling?"

Familiar? What the hell had he meant by that?

"Um." I closed my eyes as the stammered word exited my lips. Pushing my ass back against the thick, undisputable, hardness, I exhaled. "I'm not opposed to being dicked to death, I guess?" That wasn't his question, Ninny! "Yes, sorta? I don't know. I wanted to make you see that I'm not some little girl who isn't afraid to fire shots back," I admitted on shaky breaths which almost sounded like panting. Teeth scraped over my shoulder, and I didn't even try to stop myself from pressing back against him again.

"Can you even distinguish what the difference between a boy and a man is, Bishop?"

"No? I mean, I think so?"

He was definitely *all* man. The monstrous thing poking into my rear end wasn't boyish in the least bit. It would actually be a challenge to take, but I wasn't one to back away from a challenge.

"Well, which is it?" he asked, allowing me to rub against his hardened cock like a bitch in heat. I was going to hell, but all the best people would join me there.

"A cock?"

Had I really just said that?

I had.

Shit.

Could I sound any more stupid if I tried?

Probably. For the record.

I chided myself internally. It isn't a challenge. I'd felt many men when they'd grown erect, but none of them had ever promised the sinful burn that Rowan offered. The thought of being stretched wide to accommodate his thick, lengthy cock had a pulse beginning to beat at my clit.

"A man isn't afraid to make you feel the result of your naughty taunts. A boy would merely hide it behind something and pretend it never happened. You feel what you did to me, Bishop?"

Pressing his hard length against my upturned ass, he rumbled in a feral, threatening way that had my cunt clenching to accept whatever the bastard offered. Traitorous bitch was shameless. A violent tremor rocked through me as his hands lowered to the hemline of my skirt. Slowly, his fingertips raised the material until cool air drifted against my frenzied flesh.

"There's no bloody way you're a Bishop, Moira Darling. No fucking way," he hummed before releasing the skirt to grip my arm so he could spin me to face him. Angry eyes the hue of freshly-minted silver locked with mine before he snorted at my look of disbelief.

"I assure you I am." Why was I arguing with this smug, hot-as-sin prick?

The smile lifting his full, lush lips was anything but friendly, and it kind of reminded me of a villain who'd smile as he dismembered you while you pleaded for mercy.

"I swear to all that's holy, if you're a serial killer, I don't want to know. Just end me and throw my body to the bears. Don't let my sweet grandmother have to identify my remains. That's all I'm asking. There's a meadow a little way past here where you can bury me. I played in it often as a child and no one ever disturbed me there." The smile on his lips faded before he chuckled.

"If you ever touch me again in anger, it better be because we're about to fuck. Do you understand me?"

At my quick nod and terrified stare, he exhaled slowly as if fighting against the need to strangle me. His cheek was red from my hand, which actually ached from slapping his smug face. Tears began welling in my eyes as the thought of him actually hurting me sank into my exhausted, stupefied mind.

"Relax, darling. If I intended to kill you, I wouldn't have ruined the chance of tasting your lust before snuffing out that light in your lovely eyes," he admitted before stepping closer, which forced me to step back to maintain a safe distance between us.

"I should go," I whispered through the confusion warring through my mind. What the hell was even happening here? It was like we'd become flames which were drawn to one another, but neither wanted to admit it. Or, I imagined his attraction to me, which was probably because of the escapade I'd had tonight.

"I'm not the only one using scent as bait, am I?" Blinking in confusion, I opened my lips to reply, but words evaded me. His silvery eyes studied the confusion stamped on my face before he leaned in close, whispering against my ear. "Pomegranate and white lotus petals, correct? Just a few petals mixed with the forbidden fruit on a Bishop's flesh is enough to make the devil notice. I assure you of this: he's taken notice of you, Moira." His nose skimmed over the line of my jaw until he reached my chin, and then he lifted so we silently traded oxygen. "Do me a favor and don't forget to tell your be*witching* grandmother I'll expect tea with her homemade scones when I arrive at noon."

"She's sick, Rowan," I whispered with his enticing mouth entirely too close to mine. It was taking everything I had inside of me not to close the space and taste the sin he offered.

"Violet Bishop isn't sick. Is that how she got you to return?" he asked incredulously. "She's always been a crafty old bat, but I thought lying to her own blood just to force them back into the fold was beneath her. It's a pity you carry their name, even though I don't buy that you're one of them. You're entirely too naïve, pretty, and pliable, little bird." His palm brushed against my cheek before he stepped back, dropping his hand to the passenger door handle and pulling it open. "Get your stuff and then be a good girl for me and walk through the hidden entrance to the estate. Don't stop until you're at the door. This isn't the same place you grew up in. Hell's empty, and all the devils are here to play. Shakespeare may have been preemptive, but he wasn't wrong."

I grabbed my backpack and purse and then stepped back so he could shut the door. He did and then rounded to the driver's side without sparing me so much as a glance. Frowning at his odd dismissal, I spun on my heel and marched toward the ivy covering the small, hidden hatch beside an old willow tree. Yanking it open, I ducked through it as I closed the distance between me and the old manor that I'd grown up in.

The house was a large southern-style home, and in the dark, it was hard to see the ivy and dainty, blue flowers twining around the towering columns that rose to the veranda. Still, I knew they were there just as surely as I had known the supposed-to-be-secret entrance onto the property would be there. At the door, I tapped the ancient door knocker against the heavy wood three times before the familiar tune met my ears.

"I'm coming. Hold your knickers," she called out a second before she pulled the door open. Her eyes widened when she clapped her sights on me, and her lips parted as if she were about to say something, but the hum of an engine revving forced her ice-blue stare to where Rowan was backing down the narrow lane. "Moira Darling, tell me you had the good sense not to entertain Rowan Teivel."

"I went off the road on my way home. He was kind enough to offer me a ride," I stated cautiously. The look of worry on her face as she continued looking past me was worrisome. Swallowing down the sense of foreboding, I turned to watch as he drove down the single lane road until only his headlights were visible in the darkness.

"He's not for you, girl," she whispered as we watched the taillights turning toward the neighboring mansion. "That one has his own demons to tend to, and then some."

CHAPTER THREE

MOIRA

"Come on, get inside. There are demons out tonight," she whispered as she yanked me inside and slammed the door closed behind us. Inspecting me with a gentle smile creating lines in the corner of her eyes, she shook her head slowly. "You look like roadkill."

"Thanks, Grams," I grumbled, setting my backpack down against the wall in the hallway. "I missed you, too."

Her soft, blue eyes slid over me, searching for any changes since I'd left home five years ago. I'd changed a lot of things since leaving here five years ago, which I didn't regret. I'd left a seventeen-year-old girl on the cusp of adulthood, and returned as a full-grown woman. After having LASIK surgery to fix my near-sighted issue, I paid to remove the braces early and slimmed down.

"You've grown up, child." Her eyes teared up before she rubbed them. "I wish you would've warned me you were coming home. I'd have met you at the airport like I did last time," she stated, wiping the lenses of her glasses on her robe before slipping them on.

"I wouldn't make you pick me up. Besides, I drove from Boston to Idaho." Wow, did she honestly think I'd allow her to make the four-hour drive to pick me up? I wasn't an asshole, or at least, I tried not to be one. At her saddened look, I quickly looked for something to fill the silence. "I didn't end up with much from my mother, did I?" Inwardly wincing at my stupidity of words, I smiled weakly.

"You know, I always thought you'd end up with our coloring when you were a babe. But I see now why the powers that be chose to let your inner-radiance shine. You may not have been blessed with the Bishop coloring, but you definitely have the same smile and intelligence of the women who came before you, Moira. Your coloring is all from the bastard who left a deposit in your mama's belly." Slowly blinking at her blunt reply, a smile spread over my face.

"I've really missed you, Grams." No one was as blunt as my grandmother, or blasé about sex, either. I'd been embarrassed at first, but I loved it probably more than I should. The woman wasn't shy about anything. I'd learned to filter what left my lips in Ireland when I'd offended more than one pearl-clutching woman with my bluntness.

I'd left Witchery Hollow as a terrified girl, and returned

as a confident woman. When I'd left, I'd still had the braces because of an overbite, because I'd gotten them put on later than most kids would've. I'd been awkward and lanky without a hint of a figure in sight. In fact, I'd expected never to actually have one. Hard work spent in the gym, a lot of YouTube tutorials that had gone wrong, and I'd sculpted my body into somewhat of an attractive shape. Plus, my eyesight had been problematic, and I'd hated wearing the thick, Coke-bottle glasses in school. The kids had been merciless with their taunts and slurs they'd used on me. I'd hated myself more than any of them could've known. They merely added salt to a festering wound.

I'd saved up every penny I had to pay for *LASIK* surgery, then found a dentist to remove the braces. Of course, if we'd had an actual orthodontist, I'd have been out of the braces long before I was. The one who'd removed them stated I hadn't needed them

"Were there no suitable men abroad or in Boston?" she asked pointedly before heading to the hallway.

"I wasn't looking to settle down with anyone." Honestly, I hadn't wanted to live that far from my only family. I hadn't been looking for a prince charming, either. I had a tendency to pick out bad boys, or ones who'd break my heart if I let them near it, which was why I hadn't let them get too close to me.

"You do know that beauty wanes? You've got to catch

a man when you're young and nail him down. Can't steal his breath or his soul if you're too old to chase after the fella."

Her words conjured an image of her straddling grandfather as she sucked his soul from his lips, playing out in my head. Shaking it off, I laughed softly at my overactive imagination.

"I've met plenty of men but none worth bringing home." The bevy of one-night stands I'd had rushed through my head. "I just haven't found the one who gives me butterflies and takes my breath away."

An image of Rowan popped up and removed the men I'd been with entirely from my mind. The prick hadn't given me butterflies. He'd made me feel the entire zoo battling against my insides, while outright choking the air from my lungs.

"Well, you won't be finding any here."

Strolling down the hallway, I scanned the portraits of Bishop women adorning the walls. The oldest of the paintings dated back to the 1500s, but the historical line of images included every generation of Bishop women to the present. The hallway of our lineage was one of my favorite places to pass the time, and Grams had even placed an old Victorian-era chaise in the space just for me.

There was even one of Bridget Bishop, who'd been accused of consorting and fornication with the devil.

Beside her portrait, Sarah Wildes stood with her step-daughter, Sarah Wildes-Bishop, at her side. The next portrait was of those who'd been persecuted for witchcraft throughout the trials. They had hung a few for it, while others had escaped imprisonment and then vanished without a trace. To the right of the Salem portrait was the branch of Bishop women who'd helped build Witchery Hollow from nothing more than a forest into a bustling small town where families were free to practice alchemy, herbology and naturopathic medicines.

They'd fled the puritan villages and settled here in the flowing mountain ranges of the Panhandle of Idaho. The legend states, they'd settled here because of the trees, which offered them protection from persecution. No puritans dared venture into the woods filled with the unknown. Punishing innocent people being accused by others was more to their liking, or so I assumed.

Back then, the world was ignorant of the ways to heal the sick or idled. Most of my ancestors had been healers, though, so after they heard of what happened in Salem, they wanted to avoid being persecuted because of superstition. I liked to think that my obsession with nature and naturopathic medicine was a little piece of them that had been passed down the lineage.

"They were beautiful souls, were they not? But they married and settled down, which is what you should've done. At the very least, you should've brought one home for your visit and acted as if you intended to wed the poor sod."

"I didn't return for a visit, Grams. I'm moving home. You need me here, and there was no way I wasn't coming back after the message you left me," I corrected as we entered the kitchen.

My grandma was stubborn, but did she honestly think I wouldn't drop everything and run back to help her through the chemo, radiation and recovery? I'd been a much different person when I'd left here, but surely, I hadn't been that awful? Gazing around the kitchen, I smiled at the fond memories we'd had in it before I'd left.

The scent of sage and bergamot filled my nostrils as a sense of homecoming simmered and warmed my senses. Soft lighting from a chandelier of white oak offered the room light. On the far side of the kitchen were French doors which opened up into the sprawling gardens in the backyard. Beyond it, a garden filled with wondrous flowers that bloomed from spring until early fall sat, bathed in the moonlight.

Striding to the old cooking stove, she set the kettle on the burner and fired it up before moving to the cupboard and retrieving two teacups. Her silver hair was in curlers, which made my lips twitch with amusement. For a woman in her early sixties, Grams didn't look a day over forty-five.

She'd had children young and lost the love of her life before she'd hit thirty-five. In all truth, it should've aged her, but it hadn't touched her outer shell. Inside, I knew she still missed Finn Flannagan, her one and only love since childhood.

"You are home for good?" she asked without turning away from the tray she was placing things on. "I thought you had a couple more classes to finish?"

"I did, but they were merely supplemental to the degrees I already have. You know, nowadays, a woman doesn't need a man to be happy. We've evolved, and there are a lot of men here." Of course, most were the ones who'd tormented me, but the town always had more men than women. Or it had when I'd left it. "And, I'm not settling until I find it," I muttered.

"Found what, Moira Darling?" she asked, and the worry churning in her gentle, blue depths had my stomach becoming a ball of regret. I didn't want to disappoint the one person who'd never let me down.

"The butterflies. The world ceasing to exist when our eyes meet for the first time. Not being able to breathe without him. I found a lot of men while traveling through the United Kingdom, but you told me to wait for those things before settling down. I want that with someone, but I also want whoever I end up with to feel those things, too. Besides, I'll have time for that later. In the message, you said if I didn't come home, I wouldn't have time to see you again."

I didn't know how to feel about having discovered exactly that with a stranger on a shadowy highway. Rowman stopped the entire world from turning, even it went silent. He'd then made something inside of me come alive with voracious hunger to sip deeper from the bottomless well of sin he'd offered. Never before had I ever felt a connection. It left me spinning on how to handle my feelings and the response I'd had to him. I both hated and craved it at the same time, which left me reeling in a mass of confusion.

"Not everyone gets the love they seek. Sometimes, we have to take what the goddess offers. There's no one in this town who would suit you, I'm afraid. And what message did I say such nonsense in?" She sat at the table, and I took the seat across from her.

"The one where you told me you were sick."

The skin on her forehead wrinkled as her features crinkled with a look of confusion stamped over it. Her frail hands lifted the teapot to fill my cup before moving to fill her own, and the familiar scent of sweet butterfly pea flower combined with the earthy undertone of chamomile drifted to my nose.

"I didn't call you and say I was sick, Grimoira. I'd never

make you worry in such a manner." She set the teapot down before continuing. "Besides, I'm not sick. I feel perfectly fine."

Confusion shot through me as my stomach dropped. "No, you called and left a message saying you have cancer. Look, I'm not upset about coming home, but I know it was you, Grams. You told me they'd diagnosed you with an aggressive cancer and had little time left. You said if I wanted to see you again, I should come home before the end of summer. I know your voice." Panic thrummed through me, forcing me to my feet, as Grams rose with me.

"Where are you going?" she asked.

"To get my phone so you can listen to the message. Is it brain cancer? Maybe you forgot you told me about it?"

"Grimoira Darling Bishop, I'd never tell you I was dying over a damn phone call, never mind a message." Her tone was heavy with defensiveness. "Maybe you dreamed of it and thought it was real?"

I'd always had vivid, lucid dreams, but there was no way I uprooted my whole life because I hadn't been able to discern a dream from reality. Before I could insist, I hadn't been mistaken, her cool hands clasped mine and she smiled.

"No, it couldn't have been." Shaking my head, I felt my stomach sinking to the hardwood floor at my feet. "No, it wasn't a dream! Before I'd even gotten out of bed that morning, I'd called and quit both of my jobs."

"See? It's not entirely impossible you dreamt it up after all. Many people have done the same thing, I'm sure." She forced a smile, because more than likely, I was the only idiot who'd ever done it. I loved her a little more for not calling me out for being one, honestly.

"I don't make rash decisions without concrete evidence," I argued, even as she lifted one eye brow higher than the other.

"You just drove across the entire country without phoning home, first." She had a valid point, but I'd replayed the message multiple times.

Rolling my eyes, I responded. "Besides that, of course."

"Of course. You're here now and how it happened is moot. Come, sit with me and have some tea. I've missed our late-night rituals the most since you've been gone. We'll worry about the message tomorrow. Some of the girls are coming over around noon to discuss the book we've been reading. You should join us. They'd love to see you."

"Speaking of tomorrow," I muttered, returning to my seat. "Rowan Teivel said he'll be here for tea around noon tomorrow. He'd like you to make scones."

The moment my words were off the tip of my tongue, the color drained from her face. Narrowing my eyes on her hand, I watched the delicate tea cup shaking before she placed it on the saucer. The harsh sound of glass crashing together pierced my ears. Lifting my regard to the shock flittering in her eyes, my lips jerked down into a frown.

"Around noon?" she asked as she recovered her composure.

Her lips remained strained in a white line, which was how I'd always known something was bothering her as a child. It was the only way to discern if she was sad or felt any emotions at all. Grams was a tough cookie to crack. Once you got to really know her, you couldn't help but love the eccentric woman beneath the hard exterior layer.

"What else did he say to you?"

"Not much," I lied.

No way in hell I'd tell her about what he'd done to me against the car! The entire conversation with Rowan tonight was being sealed in the vault. I'd examine them and how he'd made me feel later, when I could be alone with my thoughts. Grams watched me through narrowed slits, as if she was about to call my bluff.

"Fine, Moira. You can keep your secrets for now, but only if you answer my next question honestly." The mere fact that she knew I was withholding information was irritating. She'd done it throughout my entire childhood. As if she had some way of discerning the truth by tone of voice, or something.

"Ask it then, I promise to tell the truth, Grams."

"Did you agree to do anything with him?" I shook my head, which seemed to appease her. "You didn't invite him over for tea, did you?" The tenseness of her tone was worrisome, as if she *feared* Rowan. The guy came on strong, certainly. But in all my life, I'd never known my grandmother to be afraid of anything, not even bears.

"Not that I can recall," I admitted while trying to recall if I'd accepting his strange request to tea and scones. The fact that he'd actually stated tea with scones had conjured images of Pride and Prejudice in my head as he'd mentioned them. It was difficult to recall what I'd said in response at the nonsense my imagination was dishing up at his choice of words.

That had her eyes narrowing as she slammed the teacup down and snapped back a reply. "Did you agree to *anything* else with that man? Did you accept anything from him?"

The air in the kitchen grew thick with tension. I'd never seen my grandmother angry, let alone known her to demand answers. Well, except the one time I'd gone to make-out point with Leighton Osborne.

"No," I stated softly as I placed my palms around the teacup to stave off the chill rushing through me. "Who is he, Grams?"

"He's not for you, child. Rowan Teivel isn't what he appears to be. That man's a monster posing as a saint, and I assure you that he's worse than anything you can imagine in your nightmares." The air seemed to chill a degree with every word she spoke. "I was relieved you weren't here when he returned, but it appears someone wanted you home. Pray it wasn't him because he's a blight on anyone foolish enough to trust him, but he's worse on those who are tempted by him. You're to make yourself scarce tomorrow when he comes. Do you understand me?"

"Rowan requested I be present during tea." I slowly lifted the cup to my lips and blew across the top of it as she rose from the chair once more. "Where are you going?" I was exhausted from forcing myself to wake up before the sun rose to get here early enough to sleep in a decent bed. I'd pushed myself to stop as little as possible between the red rocks of North Dakota, and the entire state of Montana in one day. The seventeen hours of mindless driving through flat, open land had been the hardest part of the entire trip home.

"To make a couple of calls," she stated without kissing my forehead, like she often did when our late-night tea time was finished. "Your bedroom is the same as you left it, but there are fresh sheets in the linen closet. Please remember to avoid the staircase to the attic. It's still missing steps, and unsafe." Pausing, she turned and leaned against the doorframe. "I'm glad you're home, Moira. I've missed you more than you can imagine. There's been a lot of changes since you left, but we'll discuss that once you're settled in. If you need anything, you know where it is. I love you."

"I love you too," I muttered to her back as she moved from the room, leaving me to finish my tea alone.

The short staircase to the second-floor didn't give me enough time to shake the foreboding feeling of Grams words, but the nostalgia of my childhood bedroom softened it a bit. I looked around the space with older eyes and perspective. Shelves were covered in lights and held empty pottery I'd once grown plants in. The four-poster bed, which had once belonged to my mother, was just as I remembered it, right down to the length of gauzy fabric and strings of lights that acted as curtains around it.

Placing my bag on the bed, I drifted over to the hammock chair in the corner, remembering how I'd insisted it have the same sheer material draped over it as the bed had. On the mirror to my vanity were a few pictures of the few friends I'd had throughout school, my mother, and pictures of myself with grams.

The room itself was painted midnight blue, which I'd loved even though Grams had pleaded for me to choose any other color. When I'd selected black, she'd caved to the blue, claiming it was the lesser of the two evils. Smiling at the memory of our argument, I chuckled. Strolling deeper into the room, I bit my lip as steel-colored eyes invaded my mind. Shaking them from my head, I moved to my nightstand and clicked on the large quartz crystal lamp before kicking off my shoes.

Then I grabbed my backpack and headed into the bathroom to shower before bed. Every inch of my body ached, and even though soaking in a bath sounded like bliss, I regretted not allowing Grams to install a shower when she'd wanted to. Not having the energy for a bath, I elected to skip it and brushed my teeth and washed face before making quick work of braiding my hair.

After stripping down to my panties, I yanked the soft, white crop top from my bag and pulled it on. The shorts were made of the same material but had delicate ruffles on the edges.

Then, instead of crawling straight into bed, I walked to the door that opened to an attached, wraparound balcony and stepped outside. The wide southern-style balcony had creeping ivy wrapped around each post, and columns leading to the upper-level balcony, as well.

Crossing over the old, wooden boards to peer out over the meadows behind the house, I smiled at the greenery visible by the moon's light. Bracing my hands on the railing, I inhaled the mountain air into my lungs, releasing it only after a moment.

This place was where my soul felt the lightest, and for

someone who felt entirely too much, it was a relief to be back home. Even if Grams hadn't left me that message, I was glad to be back here. Speaking of, I mused. Spinning around to retrieve my phone, I paused as one of the boards creaked loudly above me through the still of the night.

"Yes, I'm certain, Frances! He's coming here tomorrow morning," my grandmother hissed from where she stood on the upper balcony, directly above me. "I'm very aware of what would happen if Rowan discovers her secrets. Do you think me naïve enough to think he wouldn't enjoy ruining her?" She paused before making a disgruntled noise. "As you know, I've gone to great lengths to keep her hidden! Now, it seems as if it's all been for naught. Of course, I didn't leave the message, you dolt.

"I'd prefer she be someplace safe from harm, especially while the hunt is afoot. It cannot be stopped now. The hunt will happen with or without us intervening. There's simply no undoing what's already begun. For now, she's safe within the manor. It's the unknown which is worrying me most. He's demanded she be present during tea tomorrow. I fear his plans for her are more sinister and carnal than the sweet girl is prepared for. I should've prepared her better, but I didn't."

Remaining in place, I eavesdropped as she slowly paced above me. Her words sent confusion spiraling through me, and creasing over my brow.

"I know she's sweet, Frances. I raised her, and she's a good girl. But Teivel returning was foretold, whereas Moira's wasn't. Whoever is playing with the threads of our lives has to be ferreted out and dealt with before he figures out what she is. No, I haven't told her anything, let alone the truth. She hasn't shown any abilities of the Bishop line, and until she does, it's forbidden to tell her anything."

My pulse sped up as her footfalls moved farther away, forcing me to follow. Rounding the corner as she moved back toward her bedroom, I paused as the floorboard creaked beneath my foot. Grams' footsteps stopped as she told Frances to hold on, which had me slowly lifting my foot from the board and inching back toward my door.

"I'll call you back," Grams stated, before the sound of her footsteps retreated into her bedroom.

I made quick work of closing and locking the door, and then I leaped into the bed, yanked the covers back, and picked up the book from my nightstand. The door opened seconds after I'd pulled out the bookmark, which had *Twilight*'s Edward and Bella on it. Apparently, nineteen-year-old me thought it was ironic to use it in a copy of *Fifty Shades of Grey*, which I'd intended to donate after reading to avoid anyone discovering my love of smut.

I read *much* filthier things since leaving home. Stories that were so much darker and so much more depraved that reading even the most scandalous scene in that book wouldn't likely be enough to make my vagina pulse. I was unscrupulously wicked, but I fucking loved it and wasn't ashamed of being so. Sexuality was subjective to the person enjoying it, and I didn't care what others thought of my proclivities.

"I see you're still awake, Moira Darling." Humor sparkled in her eyes while she remained against the doorframe, scanning the bedroom.

"Yes," I admitted, before setting the book aside. "Winding down a little before I try to sleep. I got used to the noises of the city and the hard bed back at the studio apartment I rented."

"I should've come out there and seen it—or you, for that matter," she whispered as she moved deeper into the room. Smiling, she sat on my bed and picked up the picture of us together in London, then sat it down. "You should get some sleep. We've a lot of catching up to do. I'd love to hear all about your time in Ireland. You must've had so many great friends, and adventures there."

"I did," I confirmed with warmth spreading through me.

It had to be the exhaustion catching up with me. This was my grams, the woman who'd raised me without complaint even though she hadn't been forced to take on the responsibility.

"Ireland was amazing, even if it rained a lot. The library in Trinity College was pretty overwhelming to see in person. Do you know they have the Book of Kell's in it?" Smothering a yawn with my hand, I felt my eyes growing heavier.

"I've heard it's an amazing sight," she agreed before slipping from the bed. Leaning over, she tucked me in before rising to smile down at me. "Sleep well, Moira Darling. We'll have plenty of time to catch up once you're rested and settled in."

CHAPTER FOUR

ROWAN

THE SHIT I'D SET in motion was coming together splendidly. It shouldn't have been as easy as it was to call each Bishop witch home. Either Violet was weakening, or she'd become too comfortable in the hills I'd led her and her people to so long ago. I'd chosen the perfect place for them, which allowed me to easily keep track of her bloodline.

Violet owed me for what I'd done for her, nevertheless, she refused to hand over the one thing which could free me from the noose around my neck. But I wasn't planning to back down this time, no matter what happened. I'd waited too fucking long to be free of the chains binding me. Not even her very pretty granddaughter, who'd be the key to bringing her grandmother to her knees, would stop me.

When news of Rena's pregnancy circulated, it had sent shockwaves off in the Underworld. Bishop women didn't procreate without Lucifer's blessing. It just didn't fucking happen. But something had successfully bypassed the magical IUD Lucifer had in place to protect his bloodline. After meeting Moira, I was even more intrigued to figure out what genetics had created the ethereal, lithe creature.

Moira Darling was naïve, but intelligent. I'd seen the proof of it in her eyes when she'd tried to connect things together. She'd named off the classes she'd taken, confirming she wasn't merely a sex toy to be played with. Unsurprisingly, everything she'd taken would be lucrative in witchcraft, which Moira appeared to be clueless about. I hadn't believed the beguiling creature at first, but the more I watched her, the more truthful it seemed.

The girl was soft curves and sharp edges. I craved a taste of her pleasure to see if she'd be as wild and reckless in bed as she was outside of it. Her fear was intoxicating, but mixed with her arousal? Fucking delicious. Violet either assumed Moira was protected by the Bishop protection spells, or that the girl was too intelligent to end up in the hands of her enemies. Of course, she'd been wrong. I could've easily taken her from Violet without a fight tonight. Instead, I'd dropped her off on Violet's doorstep.

Entering the room, I scanned the walls as the runes hummed with warning at my presence. A smirk spread over my lips as the men noted it, groaning before returning to what they'd been doing before I'd arrived. I could read the room without them asking the question.

"I have a reason for allowing her to reach the manor. For now, she's more useful where she is, gentlemen." Grunts sounded at my answer to the burning question hovering in the air. "Violet knows I could've easily kept her pretty little granddaughter if I'd chosen to do so. Let her go mad, wondering why I didn't seize her when I had the chance." I'd been asking myself the same fucking question as well. But if I was being honest, I had something much more sinister planned for Moira.

"She's beautiful, brother," Lorne rumbled from the fireplace, where he poured two fingers of bourbon into a glass.

"Yes, very pretty and deliciously naïve about what she is," Xayden chuckled from the chesterfield he occupied. "Can we play with her?"

"No." I grunted, taking a seat beside him. I didn't like them speaking of Moira, which merely pissed me off that it bothered me at all. She wasn't mine, nor would she be. "She's different from the others. I'm not sure what it is about her, but she is. Her scent is off, but between the pomegranate and white lotus perfume, it's hard to pinpoint what is wrong about it. There's also her coloring. Never in the history of the Bishop line have any of them been born without the scarlet-colored hair or ice-colored eyes they are known for. So, who bedded Rena Bishop to create pretty little Moira Darling? Whoever sired her, he managed to break the bloodline genetics. That's something no other has managed to do before."

"That's true," Jaxon agreed as he strolled into the room and plopped down on the armchair across from me. His amethyst eyes sparkled as his lips curled into a sly grin. "Here's your little hottie before she left town, asshole." I narrowed my gaze at the picture he held up and smiled without having to fake it. "No one here's mentioned her, so I figured it needed a second look. I found this image in the yearbook for the high school. Her birth certificate wasn't easy to find. It's almost as if they were trying to conceal her parentage on it, but it was a dead-end, too." Leaning forward, he held out her birth certificate, which I took.

"Moira Darling Bishop, born to Rena Sarah Bishop on April 30th with no witnesses? That doesn't scream 'bullshit' at all, does it, gentlemen?" They did not spell the parchment like other documents pertaining to the Bishop line. Almost as if they meant it to be discovered. "There is no father listed, which marks her as impure and is a blight on the bloodline. No way in hell would Violet allow a daughter of hers to birth an impure witch into the line, not unless it was important. To my knowledge, there has only ever been one other, and that was Violet herself. This isn't Rena's signature, either. I've studied their signatures more than I've studied my own. Violet Bishop forged her daughter's name. What I want to know is, why would she need to do so? Did Rena not care enough to fill one out? Or, are they hiding something big from daddy dearest?"

Not since The Hammer of the Witches had a witch willingly taken in an impure witch. That was in 1486, which was when the witch-hunting manual was written, and they almost wiped witches from existence. "Violet still hasn't admitted to anyone here that her mother was Isobel Gowdie, or that she's the daughter of Satan." It stood to reason. No one would willingly admit they were the daughter of the devil.

Movement outside the window caught my eye, and I shifted my attention to it. Moira was outside the Bishop manor, apparently trying to hear something her grandmother was saying as she paced the balcony above her. Rising from the couch, I moved to the sliding glass doors and pulled them open, stepping outside. Studying the girl from afar, I caressed her delicate neck with ravenous eyes before forcing my attention to Violet. A smile twisted my lips, knowing she'd seen me leaving after dropping off her precious package. Whatever the old witch said had pain flashing across Moira's pretty face, and I found a certain dislike for anyone other than me hurting Moira Darling.

I'd never been attracted to a woman as strongly as I'd been to Moira. It wasn't her beauty that caught my attention, even though she was breathtakingly beautiful. It was something else, and the pull to her was alarming. I wasn't a nice guy, and I had no intention of becoming one either.

If I was a better man, I'd ignore the pull to the pretty imp. But I wasn't, and she was oblivious to the war being fought here. A war in which I'd been moving parts around since the day I'd discovered Isobel's betrayal. Too many things were falling into place already, and there wasn't a way to stop what had already begun. Besides, I had no place for Moira in my life. I'd let one woman in, and she'd destroyed any kindness I'd held.

No, I wasn't here to play with one pretty woman who got my cock hard. I was here to take back what was rightfully mine. The Book of *Daemonologie*. It was the very book that the king of Scotland told the world he'd written five-thousand-years after it had actually been penned. One lie had started it all, which resulted in the devil rising. Each witch sacrificed had brought him closer to the surface until the seal on his prison broke. The moment they'd released him from hell, Satan had targeted those who'd forsaken him. The same creatures who'd once worshipped the ground he'd walked on. Demons and witches. He'd pretended to be on our side long enough to destroy the partnership we'd created. But for some of us, it destroyed much more.

That was why Isobel had been susceptible to the devil's influence. And also, why she'd confessed to witchcraft, knowing she'd never escape the taste of flames against her naked flesh. It had given the devil enough time to find and retrieve both books. Books that the witch-hunters had stolen and intended to use to destroy both demons and witches alike. The devil had discovered the hidden tomes, and in their place, he'd planted forgeries with crucial pieces missing. The witch-hunters then circulated the counterfeit copies to the four corners of the land.

In the end, we'd merely been playing a losing game. The devil had used us in a game of his choosing and design. We'd been told to choose between sacrificing something we loved, or the original books which could protect our races. I'd chosen to save something I'd thought would be more precious to the woman who'd betrayed me.

I'd chosen what she'd created with the devil. Unbeknownst to me it had bound my hands from intervening to save Isobel. It forced me to watch as they broke her mind and body until nothing remained of the woman I'd once loved. The witch-hunters and finders had drowned Isobel in barrels of holy water. When she refused to die, they took to beating her with heavy stones. The sound of her bones shattering beneath them still haunts my dreams. They'd whipped the flesh from her back multiple times, with nary a cry from her lips for mercy. But when she wouldn't break, they violated her in ways so cruel, that she lost her mind. She'd lain there in the filth of their releases, bloodied from their brutality. I'd waited for her mind to return, but it never had.

She'd remained there, forgotten by the witch-hunters, and finders and priests. I'd refused to abandon her. On the morning of All Hallows' Eve, Isobel's scream ripped through the musky, death-filled dungeons. For hours, she'd screamed and cried, even as she forced the child she'd created with Satan from her frail, emaciated body. I'd expected something unsightly, or with hooves. But the tiny babe wasn't grotesque at all. She was the most beautiful thing I'd ever seen. I'd swaddled the babe and then taken her to a coven to be nursed and looked after. I'd protected the child from the shadows until she'd no longer needed protection from anything.

"You cannot have her, demon," Violet's voice drifted over the wind, forcing my eyes from where I'd been watching her precious granddaughter pretending to read. Her choice of reading material was questionable, but intriguing at the same time. Images of her naked and bound to the bed with red welts covering her smooth, taut skin had my dick twitching.

"If I want her, she'll be mine, witch. If I decide to take her from you, there isn't anything you could do to stop me. You and I both know the truth of it, don't we? Your father doesn't scare me any more than the insane mess-of-a-mother you hide in your crypt outside of your manor does." Her gasp of shock made my smile widen. Did she really think I wouldn't find out her secrets? "Yes, I know who your daddy is, and your mother. I was there when you drew air into your underdeveloped lungs. I'm the one who delivered you to the witches and kept you hidden from humans ever discovering you existed."

"It changes nothing, Teivel. If you attempt to claim her, I'll fight you with everything I have. This is my house, and you're not welcome inside of it. This entire place has become hallowed grounds which your kind cannot dwell within."

She stood on the balcony above Moira's, and the blatant worry and fear on her face fed the beasts within me. It made everything inside me erupt as thousands of voices echoed through my skull. It only pulled even more horror from the icy-blue eyes of the oldest witch in existence. Violet was the first witch born of a mortal woman, and the devil himself. She shouldn't have existed, but I'd fed her my blood before leaving her with witches bound to Lilith. They'd called her an abomination, which, technically, she was. Violet had no ties to the mother of witches, nor had she needed the connection they were forced to obey.

Isobel's connection to Lilith had been severed to protect

the witches from sharing her fate. As a gift from Lilith, they had promised her eternal life if she chose the witches over the child she carried. She'd intended to use her immortality to align with Satan in Hell. But she'd forgotten one important thing. Lilith was the Queen of Hell, and she wouldn't be dethroned. Lilith had gifted Isobel with eternal life, but she'd done it through creating a separate line of witches. One which wasn't bound by the laws enforced on others who wielded witchcraft.

I'd been the one who watched over the new witches. A tedious job, but one I'd taken pride from until Satan stepped in, and told them he'd been their protector and benefactor this entire time. Which was why it was time to take what belonged to me, and leave them to their fate at the hands of the devil.

"You can fight me, but we both know this only ends when you hand over what I'm here for. Until then, cease with your empty threats. And, Violet, witches cannot dwell in or on hallowed ground. You may not have emerged from Lilith's womb, but we have forced you to adhere to the same curses and weaknesses her line is beholden to obey. Now, try to sleep. We have a date tomorrow with that beautiful, sweet grandchild of yours."

Dismissing her outright, I strode back into my manor. I ignored the curious glances the men shot at me, and headed for my bedroom. I had a date with my little witch in the dreamscape I'd created for her while waiting for her to seek out her bed. Dreams were the one place that couldn't be warded against entrance. Not even Satan could prevent me from entering his. It was my playground. And I intended to play with the imp, immensely.

CHAPTER FIVE

MOIRA

THE LIGHT OF THE moon fed the meadow light from above. Vegetation crunched beneath my feet as I drifted through the soft, lush greenery. Petrichor, the scent released after the clouds unleashed rain to quench the parched earth, clung to the air. Beneath that, carried on the breeze, was the aroma of minerals and the sourness and tang of greenery. The combination forced my lips to twist into a smile because it was very much as if the rain-drunk soil was exhaling with relief or contentment.

I was dressed in a sheer material of prismatic, rainbow-colored hues, which exposed my near-nakedness to the night. Though the thin, white lace panties with bows tied at my hips were so skimpy I might as well be naked. My hair was unbound, so it lifted and floated as the breeze picked up. Tiny bumps spread over my flesh as the sound of something whispering my name was on the wind. The dark, honeyed tone was seductive and welcoming as it beckoned me further into the meadow.

I didn't resist the call, striding forward through the meadow at a leisurely pace. I knew the glade by heart since I'd often snuck into it while I'd been out collecting herbs. All around it, thick, towering pines created a barrier, concealing the slice of heaven from the taint of the outside worlds.

The closer I moved toward the center, the warmer the air became, and the thick fog rolling in off the mountains was beginning to settle on the floor of the meadow. Something about the way it twisted and danced as if independent of the wind, sent a sliver of unease through me, making me itch to turn back and run to the safety of the manor.

Even more unsettling was the lack of sound. There were no insect or bird sounds, which would typically be clear no matter the time of day. The babbling brook that flowed through the forest to the right of the meadow was dulled, but at least it was still there—a minor comfort. The hair on my nape rose with the wrongness of it all, and my skin itched with an awareness that only came when something or someone was watching me.

Spinning around without looking away from the dark tree line, I collided with something solid and unmoving. My palms landed on warm, hard flesh as a scream ripped free from my lungs, but I silenced it as soon as I realized it was Rowan.

A half-naked Rowan, to be exact.

"Scared of monsters, Bishop?" he asked in a raspy tone that grated over my delicate skin. "I hear they're ravenous for innocent maidens tonight."

"No," I returned breathlessly. "I'm not a child, Teivel. Monsters no longer scare me." Pushing off his chest, I stepped back and tried not to let my gaze drop to the gray sweatpants he wore. Swallowing the moan at the sight of him in gray sweatpants, I licked my parched lips. "Is there a reason you're wearing sweatpants? Or did someone let you in on the obsession women have with them?"

"I didn't want to seem overdressed since you're wearing so . . . little," he purred wickedly. Making no secret of taking in the tiny nightgown, he slowly returned his darkening eyes to my face as heat began rushing through me. "You look good with clothes on, Bishop. But you'd look better with those panties around your ankles and those pouty lips around my cock."

"And you'd look better with me sitting on your face," I shot back without blushing. "It's too bad neither of us will look good tonight."

"Ah, but tonight you're at the mercy of a monster," he returned. "And anyone would look better with you riding their face. You're a very pretty girl. But I'd bet my soul you're even prettier when your cheeks are flushed with pleasure." Damn, he was rather smooth. Or, I was smooth in creating a dream version of the smug bastard? Either way, I couldn't argue with what he'd said.

Under the moonlight, he looked like a half-naked god or beast. If he were a god, he'd be the one who was attached to lust, sex, or defiling maidens. Hard, sinewy lines of muscle covered his abdomen and chest. His inky dark hair was disheveled, as if he'd crawled from his bed to hunt me down. The tattoos crawling over his skin seemed to pulse with the hum of my heartbeat thundering in my chest. Rowan had full sleeve tattoos down both arms, and there was a strange, foreign dialect scrawled underneath his pecs which vanished into the tattoos painted on his sides. Lower, a prominent V-line started, then led a sinful path to the thickly-outlined cock, which was weakly concealed behind the sweatpants. I chewed my lip, considering the strangeness of the bulge, before glancing away so I didn't make an idiot of myself.

"There's no such thing as monsters," I replied.

"And if you came across a monster, what would you do? Would you invite it to taste your sweetness, or would you scream and run home like a little bitch?"

Rowan stepped closer, forcing me to cross my arms over my chest to hide the effect he was having on me. My nipples were hard, aching tips begging to be teased by his full, luscious lips. That burning need contrasted with the desire to step back, to run away before he could consume my soul. Everything inside me was alert, despite that, I didn't relent to either temptation. I didn't want to leave. It was my dream, and I controlled what happened within it. I always had, so why was I being such a little bitch? When he stepped forward once more, I mirrored him, closing the gap between us so the heat of his body wafted against mine.

A cocky smile spread over his lips as his hand slid to the small of my back, then yanked me into the hard, chiseled lines of his body. Rowan's touch made my head swim as he lowered his mouth to my ear, fanning the chilled flesh with the fever of his breath.

"Brave little thing, aren't you, Bishop?" he purred before lowering his lips to the curve of my shoulder. "You are so fucking delicate and deliciously naïve."

"I am not innocent by any means," I rebuked, as my hand slowly slid up the sinewy muscled wall of his chest. "Maybe I am the beast and you're the delicious morsel I intend to devour." I shrugged, emboldened by the knowledge that this was nothing more than a dream.

I held the control here, and I'd be damned if I cowered before him. In my dreams, I was the artist who painted the scene, and played out my filthy, immoral fantasies. I'd merely invited him here to fulfill them and use as I saw fit. The subconscious mind was a miraculous thing. The bulge in his sweatpants was hardening against my belly, which made the air catch in my lungs.

"Invite me to taste you, Bishop."

"If you wish to taste me, Teivel, do so. Don't ask permission when we both want you to do more," I whispered huskily as my tongue darted out to wet my lips.

"That mouth of yours is going to get you in trouble." His palm slowly glided up my back before his fingers threaded into my hair. The moment he had a handful, he twisted it around his hand and jerked my head back painfully. "You're about to learn why you shouldn't wander too far from home in the dark, my pretty new obsession," he growled before his mouth trailed feverish kisses over my collarbone.

The way he touched me was sure, and unhesitant. Rowan didn't ask for permission to manhandle my body, which was refreshing. He also had a mouth which made coherent thoughts die before they'd fully entered my brain. He murmured elegant words of deviant filth, loaded with depravity that painted the lewd images of him defiling my body.

Visions of lustful passion and forbidden pleasure bled into my subconscious as he continued kissing my shoulder, throat, and neck. The images spread over my soul, seeping into the darker, more indecent wantonness of my imagination. By the time he'd finished making kissing an art form, I was beyond coherent thought. Rowan was carving through my entire being as if I were an apple and he had the knife, replacing my feminine energy with that of a subservient slave to his carnal lust.

"Fucking hell, Rowan," I whimpered.

"Invite me to taste you, Bishop," he whispered as his teeth nipped my collarbone, before his breath created a blistering trail to my ear. "Fucking hell, I want to control you, command you, dominate you, and use you until you're too fucking exhausted to even breathe. Be a good girl and ask me to taste your pouty lips. Let me taste your pretty pink flesh until you're a dripping, sobbing disaster, making a mess all over my face. Don't make me ask you again," he rumbled against my ear, sending electrical shockwaves through me and causing my nerves to misfire.

"Kiss me, Rowan." The words were a barely audible breath, but at the animalistic growl he released, I knew he'd heard them. His fingers wrapped around my throat as he forced my chin up, until my eyes locked with his.

"Is your pussy wet for me? Answer me." The dominance trembling in his tone had me wishing he'd turn my throat into a fucking daycare.

"Yes." His face darkened at my sultry, whispered reply. Rowan jerked my frame against the silent strength of his solid body. I let out a husky moan as arousal began rushing to my opening. "Soaking wet," I admitted, panting through the dark, filthy shit running through my mind.

"Is this what you want from me?" His question caused the feverish breath to tickle against my flesh.

"Fuck yes," I moaned on a pant of molten need. The dark, husky laughter he released had my thighs pressing together to ease the throb he'd created.

Rowan's kiss moved down the side of my face as if he were memorizing every detail. His nose rubbed over the curve of my jawline, then slowly grazed along my pulse, which was hammering wildly. Slow, methodical touches were creating a symphony of my body, and he, the skilled conductor of it. Every kiss was calculated like a General who'd leisurely sought every weakness of his adversary. It caused everything within me to tighten into a taut, white-hot ball of frenzied need in my abdomen.

The hint of whiskey on his breath promised to leave me drunk from his kiss if he ever made it to my mouth. The hand he'd gripped my hip with released slowly inching its way up my spine, and this time, when he threaded his fingers through my hair, I craved the sharp, demanding way he jerked my head back. It gave him better access to my throat as he kissed, licked, and nipped the sensitive skin. By the time he'd finally worked his way to my mouth, I was a boneless mess of wanton flesh.

The moment his lips touched mine, the simple contact had my knees threatening to give out. His tongue traced a slow line along my lower lip, teasing me until I was almost desperate for his taste. When I moaned, he echoed it from deep in his chest, and then his mouth devoured, destroyed and debilitated any reservations I'd had about him. Our tongues met, clashed, and dueled, fighting a battle that I was just as willing to lose as I was to win. His hand on my hip released, then pushed past the flimsy material of my panties.

The way he slid a single, long finger from one end of my needy, wet flesh to the other with a feather soft touch had my insides twisting with a visceral need to be filled. I'd been touched by men in the same way, but they'd never gotten my body to respond like Rowan was right now. It had never been this erotic, and I'd never been this worked up by merely touching or kissing. Something about him had me so wild with need that I felt it literally dripping down my thigh.

There was no uncomfortable awkwardness about his presence, kiss or skilled fingers that had either of us retreating. Instead, I was emboldened to plant my hands on his sinewy, muscular chest to learn every curve and every ripple of masculine strength it radiated. Oh, so lightly, my fingertip learned the shape of the deep V of muscles that led to where the taut, smooth skin of his abdomen met the soft fabric of his sweats. I pushed beneath the waistband, found his thick cock, and was just about to wrap my fingers around it when I paused.

The warm touch of metal had my eyes popping open with curiosity, but something else that was beneath his enormous dick, brushed against my hand, and uncertainty of what I thought I'd felt wouldn't compute. The one thing I was certain of was that he had a full Jacob's ladder, but that wasn't the wildest thing inside his sweatpants.

Rowan's hand released my hair and found my wrist, stopping me from exploring further. When he twisted my arm, his mouth broke away from mine. A whimpered cry of pain exploded from my lungs as his grip on my wrist turned painful. The fingers pressing against my clit lightened before vanishing, leaving it aching for more of his touch.

"I didn't grant you permission to touch me, Bishop." The hard, icy edge in which he'd spoken had the hair on my nape rising, and his eyes narrowed, disdain churning where lust had simmered moments before. I swallowed past the uneasiness slithering through me, I licked my swollen lips.

"You were touching me, Teivel. It's only fair I do the same to you," I murmured. All emotion drained from his face, leaving me cold and bereft from the chilled air his presence created. "I'm sorry. I should've asked." The words tumbled from my lips as I stepped back, my fear turning to icy talons. "I should go."

"I don't think you're going anywhere unless I allow

you to," he stated with a deadened look churning over his features. "Pity, I thought you'd differ from the other Bishops, but you're just as easy to defile and seduce as every Bishop before you, has also been, Moira Darling." Humiliation burned its way over my cheeks, neck and chest as tears pricked against my eyes.

"Leave," I whispered thickly. "Get the hell out of my dreams, Teivel!" The moment I screamed the entire clearing seemed to pulse as if it were alive. "Get the fuck away from me now." It was my dream, and I'd be damned if he took control from me. His cocky smile had my hand moving before I'd even realized my intent. A loud *crack* echoed through the nothingness surrounding us as my palm struck against his cheek.

Before I found out if he was going to laugh or strike me back, I spun on my heel and rushed toward the lights of the manor house. The farther I got from the center of the meadow, the colder the air became, and not even the moonlight was breaking through the heavy fog blanketing the earthen floor. Something grabbed my ankle, causing me to pitch forward. I caught myself a second before my face slammed into the ground and was quick to turn over, kicking out blindly at the unseen assailant.

Invisible hands still gripped my ankle, and I bucked wildly while I tried to break its hold. A dark, wicked rumble of laughter began vibrating through the dense forest, as if hundreds of malicious eyes were gleeful to watch me struggle.

My arms were captured, and I yelped in shock when my body was rag-dolled and then flipped. Then my face was pushed into the moss-covered ground, and my ankles were jerked apart so far that a whimper of pain exploded from my lips. Fingers threaded through my hair before my head was jerked back so forcefully that pain burned along my neck and shoulders.

"What's the matter, Moira Darling? Aren't you enjoying your trip to Neverland?" he mocked, twisting my head so it forced me to look at him.

What I saw had a scream tearing from my throat like I'd swallowed rusty razor blades. All at once, I was released and the monstrous bastard vanished. I scrambled to my feet and scanned the area for any sign of him, but with the darkness and fog, it was impossible.

"I suggest you run, little doe. Because you've just become the hunted. And I've declared it open season on you." I spun on my heel and stared at the space where the manor had been. "And I'm not Peter Pan." The *tick, tick, tick* of a timepiece rose around me, and I allowed a single second of terror to freeze me in place before I sprinted toward the woods.

CHAPTER SIX

MOIRA

MY HEART WAS THUNDERING, but I didn't dare slow down or look behind me to see if he followed. The fact that I could hear his endless taunts carried on the breeze was enough proof that I hadn't lost him. The labored rasp of my wheezing breaths was probably all he needed to keep track of me.

I didn't run, period. Running wasn't fun for me, and I didn't do it if I didn't need to do so. Really, I was more of a *Netflix and chill* with some reheated Asian cuisine, girl. My muscles screamed in protest, but not knowing if he hid in one of the ghastly shadows that the moonlight cast, forced me forward at a breakneck pace.

Laughter erupted all around me, seemingly coming from every shadow and blind spot. A violent shiver shot through me as the weight of stares seared my flesh, and I slowed to a stop despite my every instinct screaming for me to keep going, to run faster.

I desperately tried to find the source of both as I

stumbled backward to lean against a tree. Somehow, the grayish-blue fog was growing thicker, more ominous as it twisted itself around and through the undergrowth. The next time the dark, husky laughter sounded, it didn't come from a dozen mouths. It came from a single one that was so close to my ear that it tickled my skin and chased goosebumps down my spine.

As I slowly turned, I expected to find Rowan there, but there was nothing but empty space and the scent of pine, moss, and earth.

"I expected more of a chase from you, Moira Darling." Rowan's deep, raspy words sounded as if they'd rebounded off every solid surface before they collided with my eardrums. "Run, little girl. When I catch you, I don't intend to leave any part of you untouched. Maybe you want me to do wicked things to your lithe body. Is that why you stopped running? Is that pretty mind of yours wondering if I'd be your filthiest, most depraved fantasy or a nightmare? The answer is both, but I promise that you'll like it either way. Does it make your lovely, pink cunt wet when you think of how I'd feel stretching it while you begged me to ruin you? I've thought about little else since leaving you at the gate of your manor. How you'd taste on my tongue, or how you'd feel around my cock. But mostly, I imagine how you'd sound screaming my name as you come for me."

Pushing off from the tree, I felt the fear growing as I stepped into the darkness. Branches scraped my flesh as I forced myself to move through them, abandoning the path I'd been moving through. The echo of branches snapping beneath footsteps caused my legs to pump faster, harder, which made them sting as the surrounding sounds began growing louder by the moment.

The wind caused the leaves to rustle high in the treetops before a shower of leaves rained down around me, even as I burst into an empty clearing. Spinning in a circle, I searched the shadows as hair-raising scratching sounds came from within them. Had I run in circles? Frustration simmered through me as I slowly treaded farther into it, as confusion creased my brow.

"Is this fun for you? Do you think this is funny?" I whirred through the chatter of my teeth as fear trickled down my spine. "What kind of psychopath thinks chasing a bitch through the woods is a good time?"

"Would it help you pretend you're not into this if I said yes?" he asked, but his voice still came from every direction. It was as if I were standing in the middle of a tunnel and he spoke from both ends at the same time. "I can smell your body's reaction to being hunted. You're not that great of an actress or liar. You enjoy being the prey for the hunter. It's okay to like it, Moira Darling."

"You're a fucking psychopath," I whispered as my

eyes rounded from the heightening of my senses. "No one enjoys being hunted like an animal." Whispers of his touch slid over my battered flesh, sending tingles of pleasure over every inch of my body.

"No? Your heart isn't pounding from the exertion, which has heightened all of your natural, animalistic instincts? Your anticipation hasn't caused your pupils to fully devour those lovely, bottle-green irises? Right now, you're searching the air for my scent because you're hunting me even as I corner you. Your primal, basic fucking nature has been forcefully evoked and awakened. Which makes everything much more intense."

While he wasn't entirely wrong, it didn't mean I wasn't fueled by the need to run *away*. I tried—and failed—to ignore the caveat that I wanted to run toward him, not away. The thought floored me as I realized I hadn't been running from him this entire time. Was I the hunter? No, because Rowan was larger and much more primal. If I was being honest, I wasn't running away. It was a dance of dominance. One I'd been losing because I hadn't known the steps to the dance before entering the dancefloor.

"Ah, my enticing prey now understands the game is afoot," he taunted. "The rules are easy enough. You run, and when I catch you, because I've always caught those I hunt, I'll decide what happens next." Every word he spoke seemed to drive my mind into a dangerously lustful state of emptiness. I didn't merely crave to be filled, pleasured, and devoured—I needed it more than I needed air in my lungs.

"Those aren't rules," I returned in a breathy pant of air. "That's like a play-by-play."

"Will having rules help?" He licked his lips as I nodded my reply. "Fine. You can't say no once you've agreed to play the game. You'll be given a short head start, but it won't help you much. Since you're new to being prey, I'll try to be gentle with you, Bishop."

"And if I refuse to play?"

"You won't."

"But if I do, then what happens?" I asked with a pulse between my thighs, confirming his theory.

"I'd keep you here until you changed your mind. Slowly driving you insane with the need to play with me. I warned you that I wasn't a good person. It shouldn't surprise you that I'm willing to play dirty to get what I want."

"And what the hell do you want, Teivel?" The voice that formed that demand must have belonged to a siren, because it couldn't have been mine.

"To give you what you want." His eyes sparkled with amusement as my thighs clenched together to stave off the ache his words caused. "You're really not a good liar. The scent of your need is thick enough I could drink it, darling.

Play the game, and I promise to ease the ache between your lovely thighs, which hasn't stopped growing since the moment I dropped you off outside your grandmother's manor."

"Fine," I conceded with an air of disinterest.

"Then there's only one question left, Bishop."

"And what would that question be?"

"When I catch you, which do you intend to take me as? Man, or beast? I assure you that there's very little difference between them anymore."

The thought of either option had arousal rushing to my slit, and my nipples pebbling so hard it was borderline painful. The idea of being ravished by some beast actually turned me on.

Admittedly, I'd always considered *Beauty and the Beast* my favorite fairy tale. However, that was because the Beast had a massive garden, library and magical beings to help me brew anything I'd want in his spacious manor. I'd never considered what I'd have wanted if he'd never returned to being a man. I mean, how desperate would I have been if he hadn't?

"Which one would be gentle?" I felt his eyes on me everywhere, caressing every inch of my sensitive flesh all at once.

"Neither," he growled huskily.

Shit, I was into this. My pussy clenched with the need

to be stretched in the way he taunted me with earlier, and I was hungry to have him make me feel wild, primal and filthy. It was as if I'd shed the weight of social constraints and allowed the devolution to twist me into something else. Something that wasn't held by rules or societal expectations and wanted to embrace every debauched whim I'd ever had.

"Holy shit," I whispered.

"I don't need to tell you what I intend to do when I catch you. You know what will happen, and you want it. That truth is evident in the sweet scent of your essence that's provoking me to give you what you crave."

He was right. Everything about me was fired up and charged to a heightened alertness. It made everything more erotic. The knowledge of him hunting me down like an animal was wicked, but also hot as fuck. I'd never thought of it in any other way than terrifying, until now. Now, I'd been shown a new perspective which had totally just unlocked a new kink for me.

"The beast," I hissed as my eyes closed and my hard, wanton panting became louder. The thrill of him catching me left me spiraling until I felt off-kilter. It simmered through my veins, want turning to need and need turning to hunger, which churned into something dangerous. *Obsession.*

A smile curled the corners of my lips as my

inner-wantonness came out to play. It flitted through my mind as the tempting scent of vetiver, bergamot and sage drifted closer. His essence was addictive, and no matter how deeply I inhaled, it wasn't enough.

Then Rowan was beside me and I was shooting out of his reach before he could claim me. Again, I raced through the forest as I dodged trees, and let myself be free from the restraint of the real world. It felt as if I was shedding the restraints of what they expected, and doing what I wanted instead.

I was *alive.*

The thrill was palpable as everything collided together and sparked, igniting the need to force him to tame me. The dark, smokey laughter whispering around me merely pushed me to move faster, harder, without relenting as shadows crept around me. I was making myself reckless by the need for him to catch me and rut me into the ground.

There was a sharp growl right behind me as I burst through the tree line. Then there was an echo of them, which was only made more unsettling by the sudden absence of the moonlight. Between one step and the next, I'd been plunged into a darkness so thick my feet faltered. The world was a void, disturbed only by the slow appearance of glowing red eyes that blinked into reality like lightning bugs floating above an open field in the summer.

Warm breath fanned my neck, stoking my sinful hunger into a feverish pitch. My thighs clenched as Rowan created a primal, animalistic sound deep in his chest, and when it exited his lips, it was a dangerous sound of need. My knees hit the ground before Rowan was there, pushing me and twisting me until my back was pressed to the damp earth. His hands gripped mine, pinning them to the ground above my head, and his nails threatened to split the delicate skin of my wrists. He knelt above me with his knees bracketing my hips, and when his features finally came into focus, a gasp lodged itself in my throat, as if it were too afraid to draw his attention.

Gone was his human face, and in its place was one of a demon. Steel-gray eyes had been replaced with black voids that threatened to swallow me entirely. Shimmering specks of silver dust moved within them, like glitter had been swallowed into the void of eternal darkness.

Towering horns protruded from his skull, spiraling gently before ending in deadly points. Behind him, huge, dark, leathery wings whispered against the air, creating a soft, gentle breeze. Veins of pulsing silver threaded over his face and flowed down his throat and arms. They hummed with an untold power, rivaling only that of the thick limbs of primordial energy dancing and surging around him. All attached to him, as if they were a part of him somehow.

Not in my wildest dreams had I ever imagined being

pinned in the drudgery by anything so hauntingly beautiful or depraved. My tongue darted out, slipping against my lips and drawing his dark, sightless gaze. I didn't need him to tell me he'd possessed me with all the power of hell driving him on. It was tangible in his energy, which promised to destroy me. The devils in hell had nothing on him, nor did incubuses.

Something pushed my legs apart, and considering his hands still pinned my wrists and his legs still caged my hips, I had no idea what that 'something' was. It ripped the thin lace gown from my body, which forced a whimpered gasp free from my lips.

Strange, magical, snakelike things slid over my belly until they teased my hard, aching tips. More of the slithering began at my ankles and worked their way up my legs before forcing my knees to bend, and my feet to flatten against the ground. The moan which broke from my lips cut through the clearing, which echoed loudly around me as whatever was touching between my thighs created friction against my needy, soaking slit.

"You should be screaming," he hissed, displeased by that fact.

He wasn't wrong. Any sane person would've been screaming until they hyperventilated. But, really, what good would it do?

None.

His feverish lips ran over the curve of my exposed breast. My eyes widened with wonder as Rowan began growing even taller than he'd been earlier. He'd become much larger, which made me look dainty and delicate compared to his frame.

"Regardless, you'll scream for me soon enough, Moira Darling."

The large, hard-to-miss cock pushing against my stomach guaranteed his claim. But, as the primal extensions of his magick that had forced my knees to bend, then began slowly trailing up the insides of my thighs, I wondered if maybe he'd get me to scream before actually fucking me.

They slid to my clit, slapping it hard enough for pleasure to rock through me, then tenderly pushed through my slick, soaked arousal. His lips captured my nipple and encased the hard tip in his fiery mouth before he bit down hard enough to elicit a whimper from the pain he'd caused.

Rowan nipped, tugged, and teased my breast before sliding his heated lips up my body to my throat. Instead of ravishing my mouth like I craved, he scorched a trail down to my other neglected nipple. When he flicked it with his tongue, my eyes widened with wonder because, holy shit, that was fucking hot.

His horns grew shorter, as if he feared skewering me

with them, and their lethal tips shimmered with glowing embers. Inky-black hands held my hips in place, but they weren't his—or, maybe they were? They were attached to him somehow, which should've had me terrified instead of intrigued. I would have fallen down the rabbit hole of possibilities, but something thick and solid which wasn't Rowan's cock, which was still resting against my stomach, began pushing against my entrance. Rowan's head lifted as it entered my pussy, pushing to invade my insides.

"Oh shit," I whimpered breathlessly.

The slithering extremity expanded, which had me moaning as it caressed, and stretched my inner walls. Then rough hands forced my hips into a new angle, giving the thing invading my pussy a better angle to delve deeper.

Rowan watched me as I watched his magical appendage fuck me. He trembled as if he felt my pussy milking it as acutely as I felt it pushing deeper.

The fact that he was letting it taste my pleasure first, confused me. I wanted him to fuck me, even if the thing caressing my walls was pleasurable. He'd warned me of his intention and that he wouldn't be gentle, but he was. And, I didn't want gentle at the moment.

The hunt had awakened something dark within me, and I'd be damned if I didn't get what I wanted. Rowan was holding back as if I couldn't handle him, which caused my vision to go red with anger. As his focus lowered to where the dark tendril slowly moved in and out of my pussy, I fought his hold on my wrists.

He growled a warning, but that only had me struggling harder to break his hold, tempting him to unleash the fervor and animalistic nature I craved. A sane person wouldn't provoke the crazed, lustful demon presently plundering her cunt. But who the hell said I was sane? Not me. Rowan slammed my arms down as the extremity fucked me hard enough to make it ache. It stroked my walls as it shifted into something with pleasuring, large bulges on the shaft, which had my whimpers turning to wanton gasps and pants.

Then I was empty and Rowan was yanking me off of the ground. His hand gripped my throat, and his ravenous mouth crashed against mine, harshly. There was no gentleness offered or wanted. His teeth scraped my lip, and his tongue invaded, demanding I concede to his prowess and dominance. As if I'd ever concede to shit. The kiss was feverishly brutal, with neither of us conceding as we went to war against one another, licking and sucking as the kiss continued until my lungs seared with the need for oxygen.

Without warning, he shoved me away so hard I fell backward, but instead of the earth and grass I had been expecting, my back hit the softness of a gigantic bed.

"I didn't expect you to actually accept a beast between

your silky thighs, Moira Darling. Earlier tonight, when I created a Neverland for you, I expected you to cry and be terrified. I didn't expect an immoral, corrupted slut to saunter in and take me so willingly."

"Who the fuck said *I* wanted to fuck you? We're not the only ones here, Teivel?" I licked my kiss-swollen lips, and only knew he followed the action because of how the thickening of silver that collected in the centers of his eyes tracked it. His lips curled into a devilish smirk before he, once again, captured my legs and wrists in vise-like grips and jerked them apart. Was I the X on a treasure map or the treasure itself? Lifting my head from the bed, I stared at the wispy tendrils sliding out from his flesh, which had captured me.

"I'm not the only one who's a horrible liar, Teivel." My words trembled from the adrenaline created by being bound, exposed and helpless. It was intoxicating to know I was helpless against him. I'd never considered being tied up with my cunt exposed would ever be anything but terrifying. But with him, it was erotic and immoral. It left me spinning in a drunken haze of lust.

"Saucy little slut," he rumbled in a deep, resonating tenor that echoed through the clearing.

The sound of growls began filling the space, and I glanced toward the woods and the crimson red eyes I'd all but forgotten about. At some point, their number had exploded from the hundreds to the thousands, and it made it seem as if the forest was ablaze.

"Pay them no attention. They're here to watch your sweet body being taken until it only ever craves what I can offer it. Eyes on me," he hissed as I felt something wrapping around my throat, forcing my eyes to collide with his. "You look at me when your cunt is dripping from the arousal I produced."

Rowan leaned down to plant his hands on the bed, and the ravenous look stamped on his features had actual fear licking through my belly. The thick, wispy, black extremities pushed down his sweatpants, revealing a *very* inhuman cock.

My eyes bulged at the thickness of it and then lowered to where the same shadowy dark tendrils slithered around it, as if they'd be adding more pleasure. The steel of the Jacob's ladder glinted in the moonlight as he gripped his cock, enjoying the knowledge of it intimidating me.

My lips parted, but when he moved to fist his cock and it . . . fucking grew bigger. Any words I'd intended to utter ended up ping-ponging inside my skull. Slowly, it continued to grow until my pussy ached at the mere thought of seating that monstrous cock inside it. The throbbing in my clit was painful, and the ball of primal need in my abdomen grew past the point of painful.

Closing my eyes, I dropped my head back to the

mattress and waited for the *Vagina-Annihilator 2000* to destroy my poor pussy. I was certain it wouldn't be the same when he'd finished sinking his cock to the hilt inside of me. That dick was a game-changer, and no way was it not going to hurt fitting it all in.

Opening my eyes, I watched him rising to stand at the edge of the mattress, watching as I moved against the things tenderly caressing me. A soft whimper slid from my kiss-swollen lips at the knowledge of what was slowly driving me to the brink of madness.

"I smell your fear, pretty girl. But your need to be fucked is overriding all else. I've never seen a Bishop spread out like a sacrifice as you are right now. Most would seek to escape the magick restraining you, Grimoira Darling."

The slithering began again, but this time, it felt unrestrained, ravenously greedy. It was all over my flesh. The rounded, wet tips of two tendrils moved over each breast and then they simultaneously clamped onto my nipples and sucked so hard, it actually hurt.

"Shit," I murmured as pleasure rushed through me. My ankles were freed but then the invisible hands returned, hoisting my knees up and apart, putting my unguarded, vulnerable sex on full display for the demon who had complete control of my body. It was becoming painfully clear that he'd mastered the most deliciously wicked art of torture possible.

"Your pretty cunt is swollen with the need to be fucked like a gluttonous bitch. I hope you're not as delicate as you appear to be." Rowan strolled to the edge of the gigantic bed.

I noted the dark tendrils detaching to remain on me, but the moment he was near enough, they latched on to him as if drawn like magnets. This was officially the freakiest dream sex of my entire life. Dropping to his knees at the edge of the bed, Rowan leaned forward to gaze at my clenching pussy.

"Such lovely, pink flesh you offer to me, Moira Darling."

Rowan's feverish breath ghosted over my sex before his tongue pushed through the mess of arousal in one gluttonously broad stroke. It slipped from one end of my sex to the other, flicking my clit with a firm, hard lick before repeating it over and over until my entire body trembled with the need for release.

His forked tongue circled my entrance before forcing its way into my cunt and making me moan so loudly that whatever beasts watching us began to growl with their approval. He wasn't even touching me with anything but his tongue, and I was teetering on the edge of blissful rapture. His wicked, husky laughter vibrated against my bald pussy as he pulled his tongue free.

"You taste like sin, but your tight cunt promises me heaven. Is that your plan? To take me to church and try to redeem my soul? Just so you're aware, I'd rather turn you into a sinner and drink from your holy grail, sweet Moira."

"Fuck no. I vote you make me a sinner and let me taste the flames of your hell." If he didn't fuck me soon, I'd be going insane. The way his eyes spread full with ink-color swallowing the white and his horns lengthened, had me whimpering at my own impending death. But honestly, if a bitch had to die, I preferred to go out being fucked brutally so I could prance into Heaven and tell them I got dicked to death. Wait, would I end up in Heaven if I let a demon fuck me six ways to Sunday?

The pressure on the bed warned me he'd abandoned toying with me, and inwardly, the thought of him fucking me until I blacked-out made me positively gleeful.

"You're going to be a rather tight fit the first time," he warned as his thick, flared-head rubbed against my pussy. It would not fit. That realization stole all my bravado and replaced it with fear. Menacing, sinister laughter told me he'd noted it, but he pushed forward, anyway.

Pressure turned to searing pain before he'd so much as nudged into me. The cry of pain I released as my body clenched tightly around his cock had whimpers coming from him, and whatever the hell was obscured within the forest. As if they were merely another extension of Rowan or some shit?

"Relax for me, Moira Darling. You're being such a good girl, taking my cock into your tight, needy cunt."

Relax? Was he fucking serious? I hadn't even taken the head of his cock, and my body felt as if it were being forced open. He pushed in deeper, forcing my walls to give way to his intrusion. The moment I felt metal, I swallowed the groan of distress and gave myself a little pat on the back for making it one step up the mammoth-ladder he was forcing me to climb.

Shit, it hurt!

Pain was forcing my body to constrict around him, so I rocked my hips, seeking to adjust enough to inch his monstrous prick deeper.

The grinding of his teeth told me he was straining, too. It wasn't until things began pulsing against my walls that my entire body shivered. His cock vibrated and then grew the same strange, rounded bumps as the other thing had done earlier. But Rowan's was geared with the metal from his ladder which added pleasure, and should've prevented his dick from doing many tricks. Or, you'd think it would?

Obviously dream Rowan wasn't human, and I was creating this version. I wouldn't be adding this dream into my diary. If I died, I didn't want anyone reading about this shit. A whimper left my lungs as the bulge began moving up and down his cock, as if it was inside his monstrous prick. While it was inside of me?

What the ever-loving fuck is that?

Did his dick just pull a Mighty-Morphin-Power-Ranger change inside my vagina? What the hell was caressing, pulsing, and licking my walls from within my pussy? My eyes clamped shut, and sweat beaded on my brow, neck and chest as he growled, pushing deeper.

"Good girl," he crooned before leaning over me and slowly pistoned his hips to create friction. Soft, delicate kisses peppered my face and throat as my loud, sultry pants puffed from my lips. "You feel so fucking good around me. Your tight pussy's milking me already, begging for me to ruin it. Is that what you want? You want me stretching it, forcing it to take all of my thick cock until it's so fucking full it aches?" He shoved in, demanding I take the second and third ladder rung at the same time, and the iron grip I had on my voice shattered.

"Yes!" I screamed and writhed against him. Was this what insanity felt like? Had my mind fractured? Who the fuck cared? I didn't—at least, not right now. "All of it, Rowan. I want all of you now," I snarled, as he shivered above me.

"All of me would rip you apart, Moira Darling." His smugness only pissed me off and offered a challenge. It was, after all, a dream, right? I bucked against him, and he growled along with the creatures attending my ruination.

He pulled back until the head of his cock sat at my entrance and then surged forward, uncaring of the burning pain he elicited. It was erotic and wrong. It was a sinful debauchery in the truest sense. It was everything. Beautiful wantonness, desirous, and carnal hunger consumed me. The feel of him shuddering as my body took inch after glorious inch drove me to crave more of him.

As he spread my legs impossibly wider and delved deeper, Rowan stared down at me with a look of ownership burning, and tightening his face. The sounds I was making changed from agonized moans to pleasurable gasps as he continued pushing in and pulling against my greedy, clenching channel.

The hands holding my hips finally released me, so the next time he plunged deep, I lifted. He froze—his base pressed against my opening—as a violent tremor rocked through both of us. Then he punched his knuckles into the mattress and lifted so he could peer down at where we were fully connected. Then his eyes slid to mine before dropping to the victorious smile curling over my lips.

It snapped something inside him, and he began pumping wildly into my body. My pleasure spiraled at a breathtaking pace while the things within me licked and caressed my G-spot, which shot me into the stars without warning. The orgasm was violent as it hammered through me with the same rough and animalistic need of the bastard fucking me.

"Good girl, you naughty little slut. You're taking all of me," he crooned. "Your pussy's milking me so fucking nicely. Such a pretty thing coming for me like a ravenous little imp." When I tried to escape the next orgasm, he was forcing me straight toward, he laughed and just fucked me harder. "That's it, fight me."

One after the other, the orgasms battered through me until my stomach ached from the intensity of them. Tears slid from my eyes as the pleasurable rapture forced them free. "You're so fucking beautiful." His hips were pistoning like a machine running on a dangerous setting and the filthy shit he whispered had my body locked in an endless orgasm.

When he sat back, his hand gripped my throat and brought me with him. His other hand slid to my hip, pulling me tight against him, and he rolled his hips. My clit throbbed wildly with the added pressure, and the creatures in the woods grew almost feral with anticipation and approval. The perverts enjoyed watching him push into my body more in this position. My focus shifted, and the hold he held on my throat tightened.

"Eyes on me, Moira Darling. Don't worry about them, they're merely a part of me," he growled, but then his entire body tensed, including the hand he had collaring my throat, and again, I was sent spinning out of control.

His name left my lips as the orgasm battered through me like a tornado spiraling through me. It sounded like a benediction that declared him my god and savior in the same breath of air. The sound of thousands of creatures moaning reached a crescendo that echoed through the night like a sympathy of pleasure.

"Fuck, you're so fucking perfect. We like you more than we expected to."

"We?" I whispered through trembling lips.

"Yes, we." He pushed me backward onto the bed, smiling devilishly down at me as he withdrew from my body.

"What the hell are you?" I asked, which admittedly, I should've done before I'd let him ruin me.

"I am Legion," he murmured while leaning forward, kissing my forehead tenderly. "And we are many. All of us have enjoyed tasting your pleasure, Bishop."

"Excuse me?" I whirred as confusion and fear shot through me.

"You didn't even wait until the sweat cooled before your mind began working."

Lifting from the bed, he clicked his tongue, which had the tendrils still caressing me slowly returning to him. After pulling up his sweatpants, he crawled from the bed without taking his eyes from me. The pleasure simmering in them as he took in the poor, pitiful mess he'd made of my vagina sent warmth slithering over my flesh.

"Now that you're ours, we have something you need to do for us. I'm going to need you to wake up, and then tiptoe downstairs, open the front door, and invite us in. Now, be a good girl for me and wake up."

I shot upright in bed, and my hand immediately pressed between my legs. There was no pain or agonizing burn, which told me that had all been a nightmare.

My brain slowly became hazy as the need to be quiet sank into my mind. The thunderous beat of my heart pounding against my ribs sent confusion clouding my thoughts until they vanished, replaced by Rowan's sultry words.

Sliding from the bed, I yanked down my thin tank top and slipped into the hallway. As quietly as I could, I headed down the staircase, careful to avoid any spots that would creak under the slightest weight. When I got to the landing, instead of heading to the kitchen for coffee, I strolled to the front door and opened it, smiling warmly at Rowan, who slid his pretty silver gaze across my face.

The sound of chairs scraping over the floor filled my ears as Rowan smiled back at me. Licking my suddenly parched lips, I giggled like some simpleminded schoolgirl. Something in my brain itched, but the feeling faded almost as soon as it took form.

"Hello, Moira." His rich, soothing baritone made my thighs squeeze together.

"Don't invite him in!" several people bellowed as a half a dozen sets of footsteps rushed toward us.

"Moira," Rowan whispered, which jerked my focus back to him. The look of masculine amusement had my brain itching as a warmth washed over me. Opening the door farther, I offered him a dreamy smile. "Aren't you going to invite me in?"

"Won't you come inside, Rowan Teivel?" I invited in a demure, velvety voice. Then a vague awareness that I'd done something wrong slammed into me, and I squeezed my eyes closed against the sensation. The hair on my nape tickled, and a chill shot down my spine, but I did not know what grievous error I'd made. When my eyelids opened again, the silver veins slithering around Rowan's eyes and his obsidian irises had me back-stepping so fast I almost fell.

"I'd love to, gorgeous," he murmured before he stepped over the threshold.

The moment Rowan entered the manor, glass shattered in the hallway. Feminine screams of horror tore through the narrow space, as if the entire Bishop line had felt the breach and wanted their displeasure to be known. Wind kicked up around me, making my skin prickle, and Rowan grabbed ahold of me. Leaning forward, he whispered against my ear.

"You are simply delicious, my sweet girl, but you're in trouble for letting me inside the one place I couldn't enter without an invitation." He shifted his attention to whomever stood behind me and added, "Poor, sweet girl. You're in over your lovely head." My entire body shook violently, as if I fought against something I couldn't escape.

"What've you done, child?" Grams asked, with tears swimming in her eyes.

"Moira's lovely, Violet—ignorant about the monsters creeping so close to your home, but exquisite all the same. Don't be too hard on the poor thing. After all, it isn't really her fault you did so little to prepare her for something like me. If you didn't want the beast feasting on the beauty, then you should've warned her. After all, it is your responsibility to keep her safe from monsters like me. Isn't it?"

"Moira isn't a part of this fight, demon!"

If she thought that was the case, then why did she look so fearful?

"Isn't she? I don't recall anyone being off-limits to me." Pulling me against the taut hardness of his body, he leaned down to whisper against my ear. "You should go get changed while I have a little chat with your grandmother. Dress in something pretty for me, but don't take too long.

We need to handle the result of our little tryst in the meadow before it can grow into an issue."

I frowned in confusion as panic slithered through me, yet still, I felt relaxed and filled with the strange, dreamlike sensation I'd woken up with.

"No need to worry. I'd never let anything harm you. At least not until I've finished with you. Now go," he stated, before giving me a little push toward the stairs.

His eyes flicked to the women and men lingering in the hallway, staring at him. When I didn't immediately start up the stairs, he cut an impatient look my way.

"Don't keep me waiting, Moira Darling. Neverland can get much, much worse if you piss me off."

CHAPTER SEVEN

MOIRA

Once I was inside my room, the dreamlike heavy haze faded, and I struggled to remember getting out of bed, which I'd obviously done. There was a throbbing ache in my temples, and no matter how hard I rubbed them, it didn't ease. It felt like I'd spent all last night partying, gotten fall-down drunk, and woke with the worst hangover of my life.

It took some effort, but I eventually managed to grab my backpack so I could find something pretty to wear. After emptying my bag and discovering nothing good enough, I froze, a frown wrinkling my brow.

What the hell was wrong with me, and why did it matter if I wore something *pretty?* I had no idea, but something in my mind demanded I do so. I glanced toward my closet, doubting anything inside would still fit me five years later, but I might get lucky.

The hinges creaked as I pulled the door open before reaching for and tugging the string attached to the light above. A deep, irritated groan escaped as I took in the assortment of clothing that hung sadly on wooden hangers. The selection of dresses was rather limited. Two of them were appropriate for clubbing and nothing else, so I grabbed the lace kimono wrap, skater mini that Aunt Katrina had sent me. It was light and airy, with a low neckline that showed a little cleavage but wasn't too revealing.

With that decided, I grabbed my toiletries and a change of undergarments and headed to the bedroom at the other end of the second-floor hallway. It was the closest one with a full shower in it.

I was in and out of the water far faster than I would've liked, but was thankful that fixing my hair and applying cosmetics didn't take long. I hoped Rowan approved of the blush-colored dress I'd chosen. The thought had me glaring at my reflection for a second before I abandoned the small, tidy bathroom and headed downstairs for tea.

As I neared the hallway with the pictures of the women in our line, my footsteps slowed. Every single pane of glass had shattered, and each woman who had been memorialized in this house since before I was born had tears of blood staining her cheeks. As I shuffled forward, careful to avoid what glass I could, I realized I no longer felt their eyes trailing me like I usually did. It was as if they'd left the house or abandoned us to our fate.

Goosebumps spread over my naked arms as I reached the mouth of the hallway, and when I turned the corner into the kitchen, what I found had me frozen in mute horror.

Everyone but Rowan was seated around the old wooden table that had an aerial view of a willow tree carved into the face. Blood filled each of the deeply carved limbs of the tree and seemed to run toward the trunk, filling it before vanishing.

"There's my pretty girl," he murmured tenderly, from where he leaned against the counter. Grams swore in a volley of obscene words at his statement, and his eyes just lit with amusement. "I'd be very careful with what comes out of your mouth next. Moira's life currently hangs in the balance. If you tip the scale, I'll walk out of here and let you deal with the aftermath of our iniquitously licentious night spent together. She's exquisite, honestly. Come here, darling." His hand extended as the other braced his weight against the counter.

As I did as he bid, I left bloody footprints in my wake. No pain touched my mind, which was almost as terrifying as blindly following his orders. It felt like a part of the dream, but I knew it wasn't. So how the hell was he controlling me? This shit didn't happen in the real world. When I came to a stop in front of him, I placed my hand into his and squealed as he jerked me against the hard contour of his body. His free hand sank into the back of my hair and jerked my head to the side, forcing my eyes toward the others within the room.

"How is it she has these pretty emerald-green eyes and ashen hair?" he inquired before his nose trailed back and forth along my collarbone.

"We're not entirely sure why her coloring isn't the same as ours," Grams whispered as tears swam in her gentle gaze. There was a plea within them, one which begged him not to hurt me. "Rowan, please. Be gentle with her. She's unaware of what we are or of what lies beneath your polite façade."

His soft huff of amusement kissed my skin. "How long do you intend to keep her in the dark? You may want her ignorant of the world around her, but I won't lie to her. Besides, I rather enjoy her pleasure and might keep her as a pet," he explained, which had a sob of horror bursting from her lips. "Your grandmother's always been overdramatic. You didn't seem to mind it earlier when I was inside you. Did you?"

A soft, needy hum escaped my lungs, and the smile he aimed toward Grams was so cold I felt it in my bones.

"See? She's lovely in every way that matters. I think she'd make an enchanting addition to my collection. Moira Darling's body was a feast I gorged gluttonously on."

The hand wrenching my head to the side released my hair and moved to my ass, gripping a handful. His eyes widened as a wolfish smile played on his sinfully delicious lips.

"Naughty girl," he hummed. "As I was saying, she's fucking delicious."

"You cannot have her, demon." The people behind me hissed vehemently.

Rowan chuckled before catching my gaze again and holding it. "Get on your knees, Moira." Without questioning it, I lowered before him, bowing my head. "Bloody hell, she truly is exquisite." He bent, grabbed my jaw painfully in one hand, and forced my eyes back to his. "Who's pretty, new toy are you?"

"Yours." My voice left the tip of my tongue in a layered tone that seemed to belong to someone else.

Shock widened my eyes, and a shudder of fear ushered in the sensation of pins and needles pressing into my brain. Pain tore through my middle, and as I wrapped my arms around my stomach and curled in on myself, a scream tore from my throat. I was being sliced open from the inside.

"That would be the consequences of our liaison in the meadow, I'm afraid."

The way his eyes softened, worried me. But before I could question it, he was straightening and walking to the sink. He came back with a glass of water, which he set on the counter before giving me a smile that was tight with pity. In his other hand, he held a wicked-looking ceremonial blade, which he used to carve a deep slice into his palm. Then the blade was gone, and he was forcing my head back and holding his bloody palm over my lips.

"Open that deliciously wicked mouth of yours and stick out your tongue."

Dutifully, I did as he bid, but my obedience chaffed something deep within me. As his blood dripped over my lips, something else clawed beneath my flesh. His eyes widened, and his lips parted as he hissed.

"What the actual fuck?"

My vision sharpened, becoming crisper and clearer. The sounds of the insects outside buzzed loudly inside my head, echoing off my skull. A horn blared on the highway five miles away, and I could smell the driver's rage before he gunned it. Passing the slower car recklessly, while screaming profanities out his window causing the other car to veer off the road to avoid a collision. Heartbeats thundered wildly around me, which I could easily locate. But my focus remained locked on the man who'd awakened something within me last night. As if he'd altered me somehow through the dream we'd shared.

It had been a fucktastrophy of a night and it was bleeding over into the day as well. I'd definitely seized the wrong fucking night to let my hair down and fuck around with the beast. He hadn't even come with a damn library! Licking my lips, his eyes narrowed as I pushed up from the floor, ignoring his desire for me to remain at his feet. The air exiting my lungs was ragged and labored as I growled through clenched teeth.

"The fuck did you do to me?" I demanded, rage churning through my vision.

"What the fuck did you do to her?" Rowan demanded as he glared at each man and woman seated at the table. Every one of them seemed just as confused as they were terrified. "Aw, shit. You don't know what the fuck your daughter created, do you?"

Rowan's blood was dripping from his fingertips, and when I inched closer to them, his soft, gray eyes slid to me. Did he know how desperately I wanted to pull his bloody fingertips into my mouth and suck them clean? Everything inside me screamed for more, to taste him until I'd consumed each of his sins.

The way he took in my face made me wonder if the weird sex dream had altered him as deeply as it had altered me. I moved to reach for him, but when I caught sight of my skin, my hand trembled.

Shimmering, iridescent veins of silver pulsed beneath my flesh, curling in tendrils to the tips of my fingers. As I watched, black lines wove through the colored ones, slowly turning the soft, delicate shimmer, murky with its darkness.

A scream ripped from my lungs as I bent over, dropping

to my knees as pain tore me apart from within. Rowan's powerful arms hefted me off the floor and cradled me as he left the kitchen. Not a single person, not even Grams, tried to stop him, and all the while, it felt as if something was trying to tear me open from the inside so it could escape the cage of my body.

"Breathe, Moira. You're okay," he assured against the crown of my head, carefully rushing up the narrow, ancient staircase and then kicking my door open.

I didn't ask how he knew which room was mine because when he set me gently on the bed, my back arched from the intensity of the hellish pain ripping through my middle.

"What the fuck is inside me?" I demanded as sweat coated my skin. If this were a horror movie, I'd guess I was shifting into a werewolf and the pain contorting my body was from my bones breaking and rearranging.

"You probably don't wish to know what's within you, darling," he stated as he scratched his neck and lowered his eyes to my exposed thighs.

A sarcastic huff of a laugh fell from his lips before he turned and strode to the bathroom. The sound of water running caused my parched mouth to fill with saliva as he returned with a glass.

"Drink this, and open those pretty lips once more. It appears to be farther along than I'd expected. Our little rendezvous in Neverland seems to have left you . . . in a rather *delicate* predicament."

"What the fuck does that mean?" I snarled before grabbing the glass and draining it in greedy gulps.

The pulsing ache rounded my body from my spine to my stomach, and the empty glass fell from numb fingers.

"I'm going to throw up," I announced, and he backed up, staring at me with wide, terror-filled eyes. "I'm going to throw up!" I demanded pointing at a small trash bin beside the shelves for my plants.

Rowan grabbed it and pushed it under my mouth as I began vomiting onyx-colored liquid.

"Bloody hell." He muttered as I continued to vomit.

My body contorted and then undulated as something thick and solid pushed up my esophagus. I gagged, choked and tried to vomit up whatever was slithering up my throat while hands stroked my hair and ran down my spine.

Rowan offered softly-whirred encouragements that did absolutely nothing to distract me from the fact that something pushed at the entrance of my throat, wiggling like a magical snake.

I couldn't take it anymore, and out of desperation, I shoved my fingers as far down my throat as I could and yanked on the slick, slimy bastard. With wide, horrified eyes, I tasted brimstone—or rather, tasted the way brimstone smelled—as the thing began to fight against my hold.

"What in the hell is inside of my granddaughter, Teivel?" Grams' anger was palpable, even as she waited for his reply.

"Get out, or die." His focus never shifted away from where I struggled to pull whatever was inside me, out, and after another second or two, his eyes bled from steel-gray to black, sightless voids and he said, "If you hurt her, I'll end you before you ever take your first breath."

Was he talking to me, or was he having a conversation with whatever was stuck in my throat? I tried to ask, but it was impossible to get words out when you had a snakelike creature pressed against your vocal cords.

"That's because it isn't supposed to come out of your throat, darling."

Did he expect me to shit it out? No, he expected me to give birth to it. But apparently, he'd missed my uterus or some shit? I couldn't even understand how it would move from my vagina to my throat. He flinched when my expression filled with horror and my face went bloodless.

"Frolicking in the meadow beneath a full moon has consequences, Moira Darling. It would seem you're compatible with me, which wasn't something I expected." He glanced at Grams, who was still frozen in the doorway. "Normally, my blood would've ended it before it could be born. To demons, it's poisonous."

"You shouldn't have been touching my granddaughter at all, Teivel. She's not part of our world, nor has she ever displayed any ability to live within it before tonight. It's forbidden for anyone or anything other than kin to introduce a blood-born daughter of darkness to her craft. You've broken the laws of magick by touching Satan's great-granddaughter without first seeking permission. Unlike the others, she's of his blood."

What in the actual fuck had she just spouted? Had the entire world gone backwoods bonkers while I'd been away at school? Leaning back into the arms of the man who'd planted the slippery sucker into my body, I whimpered and began convulsing.

"She's dying!" Her voice broke as the words slipped free.

"No, she isn't, but you will be if you don't leave this room. I won't ask you again. In order to save her, I have to open myself to accept it, which means you're fucking leaving so that I can save her life. The same as I did for you and those you've begged for me to save from being removed from this plane."

The air grew thick with tension as she refused to leave, and he refused to act while she remained.

"Her father's blood will ensure she doesn't die. If you had even half of the intelligence you pretend to house in that pea-size brain of yours, you'd have realized what your daughter carried."

"And what is that?" she whispered through tearful eyes.

"Figure it out for yourself, witch," he seethed, and something slammed against the door before screams erupted in the hallway.

Blinking as I tried to process what was happening, the door slammed closed, sealing me inside with Rowan as his arms tightened around me protectively. It was the last thing I saw before my lashes dusted against my cheeks and Grams' footsteps retreated down the hallway.

"I need you to be brave for me, Moira Darling."

His arms tightened around me, both hands sliding to where mine continued gripping the thing in my throat, fighting to yank it free. Choking on the bile, I struggled in his hold as he made soothing noises.

"It's my turn to try." His voice, which sounded soothing to my ears, boomed through my mind. The multilayered tenor soothed the demon within me, and it went still. "You've already damaged her pretty throat, so get the fuck out or I swear to hell I'll rip you out of her pretty cunt."

My eyes opened as I jerked forward, spewing the long, slippery snake-shaped demon that had burst from my lips. I stared in horror at where it slithered and flipped about like a fish out of water, and then, just as I tried to convince myself that it was over, my stomach churned and contracted sharply before expelling what felt like hundreds of smaller versions of the first one from my stomach.

"Bloody hell," Rowan whispered. "You've got to be fucking me." His arms wrapped around me and forced me back into the heat of his body. "I've got you."

"This isn't real," I whispered brokenly. "Right? This isn't happening. It can't be. I'm still dreaming."

Burying my face into the heat of his body, I shook with giant, full-body sobs. Rowan held me tightly as my body continued shuddering with sobs. His hands stroked, petted, and caressed me until I'd almost fallen asleep in his arms. The creaking from the door being opened caused my eyelashes to part as light flooded the room.

"Is it over?" Grams asked, peering at me with concerned blue eyes.

"It is, but you need to tell me how the fuck she just birthed seventy-two goetic demons," Rowan growled. "I'm also certain she just removed the magical seal from the Ars Goetia, which should have been impossible, even for me."

"I don't have to explain her to you, Legion. The only thing you need to know is that she carries my bloodline within her. No matter what Rena fucked, or created, Moira's a Bishop. Besides, it wasn't as if Rena was forthcoming with whatever she'd slept with to create her. My daughter's been excommunicated and isn't likely to return with answers." Turning my head, I peered at my grandmother in confusion. "She's dead to us either way, child. Rena abandoned her daughter in order to live her best life, at the end of the day, she left you. A Bishop never abandons their daughter—not ever. Sons are born human and sent to *him* to be trained, but our daughters house magick and must be protected."

"This is the worst acid trip of my entire life. I don't even remember taking the shit this time, but I'm certain there's a plausible, sane explanation for what is happening here." My body went numb, so I sank deeper into the arms, cradling me. "Check the tea. Maybe the leaves were bad?"

"You can leave now. This is my house, and she's my blood-born kin, who I'll tend to and ensure she recovers from what you've done to her. And, Rowan? I am her family, and I will be the one to give her an introduction to both magick and witchcraft. So mote it be, as their magick is always stronger when taught by one related through the bloodline."

Lips brushed my forehead before Rowan slowly laid me down on the bed. "Meet me in Neverland, Moira Darling. I'll be waiting for you." He smiled at me before tucking the wild strands which had fallen into my face as he'd moved me.

CHAPTER EIGHT

MOIRA

A MOAN BURST FROM my lips as consciousness slowly returned. My entire body felt beaten, bruised and wrong. Forcing my eyelids to part took effort, which resulted in a loud whimper of muffled, raspy complaint. The sound of rocking told me that Grams was in the room, but she hadn't brought her rocking chair into my room since I'd gotten drunk at a kegger, which had resulted in my being hungover for a week. Grams hadn't left my room other than to make broth, shower, and turn away my friends who checked in on me. I'd regretted drinking that night, but she'd nursed me back to health. Squeezing my eyes closed, I tried to even out my breathing to feign still being asleep.

"Pretending to be asleep won't make me go away, Moira Darling," she chided.

"Why does it feel like someone beat the shit out of me? I don't remember drinking last night," I managed to get out despite the burn in my throat. It felt as if I'd swallowed a razorblade and then chased it with lemon juice and sulfur. "My throat hurts. Did I end up sick?"

When I tried to piece together my night, none of the memories made any sense.

"It would appear you've been fornicating with a demon. Yesterday, you had to deal with the repercussions of your tryst with him." Her matter-of-fact tone had one of my eyes opening just so I could make sure she hadn't grown another head or been replaced by a pod person. She looked exactly the same as she had when I'd shown up last night, minus the curlers.

"I *fornicated* with a demon?" The amusement I'd aimed for hadn't been revealed in the tone issued from beneath my dry, cracked lips. "I'm going back to sleep." This shit wasn't happening. It couldn't, because demons didn't exist!

"No, you're not. You're going to go shower, and then you and I are heading into town. Today begins your introduction to witchcraft and magick. What Rowan Teivel did yesterday? It broke the laws of magick. The powers that be will be hearing about it soon enough, but I refuse to let him be your guide through your awakening." The chair scraped over the wood floor as she rose from it, then yanked the blanket from where I'd pulled it up to my neck. "Up with you, Moira. Magick waits for no one."

I couldn't have heard her correctly. Right? The only

proper explanation was . . . I'd died. That was it, which sucked. But, considering everything I could recall of last night, well, it was insanity. I'd dreamt of having the wildest sex of my life, then woke up to him controlling me. After that, I'd been his plaything, who'd hung on his every word. That was before I'd thrown up whatever he'd planted inside me from the wildest sex, ever. So, in conclusion, I'd died on the highway and entered some weird sort of reality. Maybe it was the in between? The world where you were forced to linger before heaven opened the pearly-white gates?

"I think there's something wrong with my hearing, Grams. It sounds like you're saying magick, witchcraft and demons? So, either I died on my way home and this was a *Beetlejuice* situation, or you've lost your marbles because the cancer is making you hallucinate. Neither one of them sounds ideal, which means I'm protesting moving from this bed. In the iconic words of Green Day, *Wake Me Up When September Ends*."

"It's June, darling."

"Exactly," I muttered while trying to come up with other explanations for this lunacy. Maybe Ashton Kutcher was about to jump out of the closet and tell me I'd been Punk'd. Afterward, we'd join Mila downstairs to watch *That '70s Show* reruns, and throw popcorn at the television set. Because what in the hell was even happening right now? This wasn't real life. It just couldn't be, right?

"Our last name's Bishop, and they've accused every single one of our descendants of witchcraft. You didn't think that was odd?"

"Of course, I did, but you told me witches weren't real, remember? You called me silly and then sent me outside to play with the other kids. What was it you said every time I so much as mentioned a connection to any of the women in our bloodline being witches? Oh, yes. I remember. 'The jealousy of women who either falsified or unjustly accused other women of witchcraft was the building stones on which they built witch trials. Men, however, merely enjoyed lighting a bitch on fire after she'd roasted him on the size of his lackluster wiener.'"

"It wasn't entirely a lie, though," she said defensively. Pushing up from the bed, I winced with the subtle movement, and then my stomach rumbled, which resulted in a soft bubble of a burp exiting my lips. The acerbic stench of sulfur hit me, making my eyes burn and Grams to lean away from me a bit. "Oh, that's disgusting." Waving her hand in the air in front of her, she made a sour face. "Well, it all comes from frolicking with demons. Isn't that what Rowan said?"

Images of the meadow we'd "frolicked" in slipped through my mind with vivid clarity. It had been a nightmare, right? Then why could I physically feel his touch on my flesh and remember how exhilarating it had been? I'd never felt more alive than I had with him touching me, fueling my arousal until I'd shattered into a thousand tiny, broken shards of glass, which he'd then carefully reconstructed into something else.

"Holy shit," I mumbled through quivering lips. "Neverland."

"This isn't a fantasy, and he isn't Peter Pan. He's *Legion*, the commander of legions of demons who dwell within his soul. Each one is a part of him, and there's no separating them. He's after something that could change the world if he were to ever get his vile, wicked hands on it. I understand he's rakishly handsome and hard to resist, but you must resist him all the same."

"No, you're right. He's definitely no Peter Pan," I agreed. He'd be more apt at playing a villain, and just the idea of him being wicked had my pussy slick and needy. The bastard had driven his cock into my pussy with immoral, unrestrained carnal ardor.

I hadn't even known my concupiscence could reach those heights until he sent me careening into the stars above our own, salacious version of Neverland. Or, I assumed, it was Neverland since he'd told me to meet him there? And, yes, I'd technically been the one to force his magnificently strange cock deeper into my body, but damn, had he come unhinged once it sunk in all the way.

In fact, I had phantom pains just thinking about how much he'd stretched, and owned every inch of my insides until I'd gone mad from it.

It was just about an hour later when I walked downstairs and spotted my rental car sitting in the driveway. Scratching the back of my neck in confusion because I hadn't called a tow truck to pull it from the ditch, I started outside.

The gravel crunched beneath my sandals as I strolled toward it and took in the new windows, pristine interior, and unblemished front bumper. The shock was so potent that I almost missed the envelope propped on the steering wheel. There wasn't anything written on it, so I assumed it was for me and ripped it open.

There was a single sheet of thick stationary tucked inside it.

I figured you'd be dealing with enough this morning and didn't need to fret over your rental car or belongings. The repairs have been paid for, and your belongings are in the trunk and remain untouched. I hope to see you in Neverland, as I'm certain you've many questions you need answered. Your grandmother will tell you I'm a monster, Moira Darling, and you should believe her because I am. I've never apologized for being a monster, and I never intend to do so. If you'd like the answers to any of the other questions swirling inside your pretty head, then meet me in the meadow. I won't promise to be

on my best behavior, since my best behavior would likely still
be sinfully immoral in your pretty, emerald eyes. Don't keep
me waiting too long, darling.

Signed by the man whose name you'll be screaming later,
Rowan Teivel

His complimentary close had a blush creeping over my
cheeks and down my neck, and if I closed my eyes, I
could still see him between my thighs, licking through
my drenched pussy. With all the men before Rowan, I'd
never felt the intensity or the satyriasis he'd radiated in his
need to devour me. It was almost terrifying how easily
he'd turned me into an addict for his depravity.

In high school, I'd more often than not gone after the
bad boys I'd known would hurt me in the end. Grams had
said it was because I was a rebellious child, which made
sense. She'd told me it was the devil's gleam in my eyes
that warned of the unruly defiance to conform to what the
world expected me to be. But the moment Rowan touched
me, I'd bent to his every dark and deviant request, demand,
and desire. Even now, I was soaking wet with the need to
feel his rough hands running over my naked flesh.

The front door opened, and I turned to find Grams
coming down the stairs. She was dressed in a black,
ankle-length skirt that brushed the tops of her soft,
leather sandals, and an over-bustline sweetheart corset of

shimmering silver, midnight blue, and onyx covered her ample cleavage. Her silver hair was braided into a bun, which was held atop her head with lengths of quartz and iron. Several charm necklaces hung around her neck, each one clanging against the next, and even more bracelets adorned her wrists.

I slid the message into my skirt pocket and then smiled as she came to a stop in front of me. "I thought you said your car was wrecked?" Her eyes slid past me toward the vehicle.

"It was," I admitted, not really wanting to explain how it ended up here and undamaged. "It seems someone was kind enough to tow it here for me, so I didn't lose my deposit on it. I'm just thankful to have one less thing to worry about today."

The huff of annoyance told me she knew exactly who the 'someone' was, but I didn't offer any affirmation or denial to her silent judgment. After another moment passed and she was convinced I would not crack, her gaze slid down the billowy shirt I wore and then to the sheer, spaghetti-strap camisole and lacy bralette that were clearly visible beneath it.

It was unseasonably hot, and there was no way I was going to sweat my ass off in her old, 1950 Chevrolet 3100 pickup truck that lacked seatbelts and air conditioning. Not that I didn't love her truck, because I did. Some of my fondest memories were made in the truck papa had restored into her dream car. I'd loved listening to her reminisce about the details and all the special touches he'd put into it just because he adored her. Their type of love was my end goal, and it had been since I was old enough to understand how unconditional and easy it had been for them.

I slid onto the soft, white leather bench seat and adjusted my skirt before yanking the heavy door closed. After rolling down the window, I placed my elbow out the door and leaned my chin on it, staring out at the meadow filled with wildflowers.

"I think they bloomed because they sensed your return, Moira. That meadow has been nothing but greenery without a blossom in sight since you left the manor. As much as I fear you being near to him, I'm glad you've returned home." Smiling, I turned to face her.

"I've missed you too, Grams. I can't wait to tell you about the things I've learned and the people I've met. You'd love Ireland. It's so magical." Her smile faltered before she laughed and slowly nodded.

"I can imagine it is, darling." Sometimes, I really thought it was such a shame she'd never left the States, but not once had she ever expressed the desire to travel. "If you need more rest, I suggest you do it before we reach the others. It's going to be a bit of a drive up to the peak of the mountain."

Despite her suggestion, I didn't nap, and the drive was quiet and left me time to think. When the truck downshifted and then idled, my eyes slid to the thick forest around us.

"It's time," Grams stated, but I was too transfixed by the hooded figures standing in the brush. There were even more figures behind them, some of whom carried lanterns with flickering candles in them. Still others, the ones who wore crimson and were interwoven with the hooded figures that had my blood turning ice cold in my veins. The air thickened with tension and something else I couldn't define.

"What is this?" I demanded in a sharply whispered hiss.

"This is your awakening to magick, Moira Darling. It's time to see how powerful you truly are. Come, my father's waiting for us."

"You've got to be fucking shitting me. Don't get out of the truck, Moira. This isn't Wonderland, and you're no Alice." Staring at the figures lingering in the woods, I felt a shiver rushing down my spine as fear churned in my abdomen. "Today is not a good day to die. I knew I shouldn't have got out of bed."

CHAPTER NINE

MOIRA

I GLUED MY ASS firmly to the seat and wasn't budging. Staring at Grams, I opened my mouth and then closed it loudly because words seemed to have failed me. Wasn't she a little past the point of a midlife crisis? Was she on drugs? Did people her age *even* do drugs? She wasn't *that* old, but I could recall smelling weed a time or two when I was young, so maybe that was it.

"Come, Moira. We don't make the devil wait. It's rude." She hummed as she exited the truck, but I just stared after her, doing my best impression of a fish out of water. After she'd taken a few steps, she glanced back to see if I was following, which I wasn't. "Now!" she snapped.

This was how I died, I decided as my fingers pulled the doorhandle. I felt it in my bones. Stepping out of the truck, I exhaled a shaky puff of air. The moment the door slammed closed behind me, chanting began. Every sane mind cell I had left demanded I run, get the fuck off the mountain, and keep going until I was far away from here.

I'd never been surer about anything in my life than I was about this. If I didn't leave right this second, I was going to end up tied to a stone altar on a mountaintop, which would result in my making headlines as the unfortunate soul whose grandmother had sacrificed her to a nameless god.

"Grams?" I hissed through teeth that chattered harder the louder the cult-like assholes chanted.

"Shh, you must remain silent until He speaks."

"Who the hell is *He*?"

"My father, who's also the devil."

I stopped dead in my tracks, unable to do anything but stare at her as if she hadn't just straight-up said her father was the *devil*.

"Um, excuse me? But did you just say the devil is your daddy? Like, he got busy with your mother, and nine months later, you strolled out of her . . . lady parts . . . because, well, Grams?"

I looked through the hooded figures who remained in place, chanting their eerie hymns of doom. Had she actually left me with the crazy cult people? She wouldn't do that, right? Fuck!

"Grandma? I'm not stepping a single pinky toe into these woods. I've seen enough horror movies to know not to enter the damn woods! I mean, really? My father's the devil, but it's okay. Come on in, little girl! We've got candy, free books and Wi-Fi? I mean, where's the white van with the shitty spray paint job? Or, did you think more like there's an altar with your name on it, written in the blood of the last stupid virginal bimbo who was dumb enough to follow me into the creepy ass woods! This entire scenario just screams 'bad fucking idea' all over it!"

I huffed before a deep, richly accented baritone whispered, "A virgin cannot be a bimbo, love."

Sure, I jumped out of my skin like a ninny, but by the time I turned toward the speaker, I'd collected myself enough to at least roll my eyes.

"It's an oxymoron thing, and for the record? I'm totally not a virgin. This pussy has been fucked a lot. So much that the devil wouldn't want it, understand?" I asked.

Had I just stated my pussy had been fucked a lot? Replaying what I'd said, I realized that, yes, I had just said that, but then I shrugged it off because it's better to be loose of morals than to be dead because they thought you were a virgin and sacrificed you to the gods, right?

"I doubt your great-grandfather would use it even if it were virginal, Grimoira," he purred as eyes the color of freshly-sprouted grass slid over my frame.

"What a relief?" I shot back sarcastically.

"That's not to say I wouldn't wish to taste of the magick your pretty soul promises to house."

"Great." I huffed before turning toward the sound of

drums beating in the distance. "Oh, drums are never a good sign."

It was like the first item on the list of doom and gloom. My heartbeat echoed the thunderous sound as the chanting cult lemmings started moving toward the bright flames visible through the foliage.

"Don't go toward the light, Moira." My voice escaped my throat weakly.

If I'd been smarter, I'd have taken my own advice. Sad, really, because I didn't. Instead, I inched down the heavily wooded path, ignoring the branches scraping over my arms.

Once I'd passed the lines of trees and inched from their protection, I found naked men and women dancing around a large, blazing bonfire.

Black tendrils wafted around them as they chanted and moved while the firelight painted their naked forms. Idiots! Weren't they afraid that their nether regions would catch fire? They should've at least waxed first, right? Was I overreacting?

Maybe, but it wasn't every day that I saw naked people dancing around open flames.

The men knelt as the women's arms lifted to sway and move hypnotically in the air. Sparks from the fire erupted into the sky, and their heads dropped back as if they were drunk on the feeling of being uninhibited in the middle of nature. The way they moved was erotic and soothing at the same time—right until my gaze landed on a large, flat stone that resembled an altar, anyway.

Maybe if I didn't look at it, it would go away.

Seemed reasonable enough, so I dragged my regard back to the women, and as I watched them, my pulse slowed. They began moving in a way that I wasn't able to fully process, but it looked almost like someone was bending each woman backward by their hair, making their bodies contort in ways that teetered on falling backward without actually doing so. The women's mouths dropped open on silent moans, only instead of sounds of pleasure, inky smoke poured from their throats.

"Fuck this shit," I cried out in horror. I spun and began running blindly through the dense forest.

Altar.

Inky smoke exiting mouths.

Heads bent at angles that should've broken their necks.

Did they really expect a girl to stick around and find out what was happening?

Nope! Not this girl.

Not today, Satan. Literally! My lungs burned as I barreled down the hillside, bypassing my grandmother's truck and the clearing altogether.

I ran like the devil was chasing me. Hysterical laughter was bubbling up from my lungs, which ached from the sharp, shallow inhales. Still, I refused to stop, forcing my arms to pump harder and my feet to keep moving.

The fiery pain in my thighs was agony, but I'd trust-fall off a cliff before stopping my mad-dash. I continued through the foliage, silently praying for someone with some semblance of sanity to appear and save me from becoming a sacrifice that ended up in a cold, unmarked grave.

When my feet hit the asphalt of the main road, I paused long enough to listen for anyone who might be following me, and the hum of an engine met my ears instead. Yup, I'd seen this horror movie too. Evil cultists had hopped into a car and were trying to intercept the poor, virginal bimbo just as she started to think she'd made it to safety.

So, I began running again. I raced the sound of the horses blasting down the country road as my body protested every step forward. At a narrow creek, I didn't pause long enough to verify I wouldn't end up drowning before I launched myself off of a rock. The moment my feet landed in the icy water, I sank up to my ankles in silt and shrieked. Falling forward into the water, I tugged on my legs to free my feet and then, cursed when the mud kept my sandals.

By the time I'd escaped the mud, I was soaking wet and barefooted, but there was no way I was stopping. Thistles and thorns bit into the soles of my feet, most of them sinking deeper into my flesh with every step. As I broke free of the forest, I skidded to a stop, gravel and tiny pebbles adding themselves to the list of things I'd be pulling out of feet if I survived, and I stared wide eyed at the car idling not six feet from me. The horn blared as a soft exhale of shock escaped my lips.

"Fuck," I whispered a split second before something slammed into me.

My body collided with a hard, unforgiving tree, and my breath left my lungs in an explosion of air. Several of the lower limbs had broken under my impact, and one of the spikes still attached to the trunk was cutting into my flesh.

I was so busy gasping for air and trying to blink through the pain that I couldn't remember when the man with eyes the color of freshly spilt ink appeared in front of me.

The scent of oak drifted to my nostrils as it warred against sage, vetiver, and bergamot. Hands cradled my face as I opened my lips to tell him what was happening, but little more than sobbed, half-broken words fell from them.

"Grams . . . *devil* . . . altar . . . I almost died!"

Rowan stared at me as if I'd gone insane. It gave me hope because cracked was better than the reality of it, and I flung myself into his arms. He'd saved me. His hands pushed the wet hair from my face before he began making soft, comforting noises against my ear.

"Can you walk, darling?"

"I have thorns in my feet," I admitted through a hiccup. "I think my Grams was going to sacrifice me to some unnamed god. I'd have made the news as some poor girl who'd been murdered by her own grandmother! I don't understand why she would do something like this? You know, you expect people to change if you haven't seen them in five years, right? Right. But to come home and have your own grams, who raised you and loved you, try to off you? I didn't sign up for this shit. Do you know she actually told me her father was waiting for me? And get this! She said her father was the devil! Can you believe that?" I asked, and he paused the heavy petting of my hair and looked over his shoulder. He didn't seem upset about anything I'd just stated, either.

"He's actually here?"

I literally felt the blood leave my head so quickly my vision tunneled.

"Oh, darling. Please don't do that," he murmured, guiding my head to rest against his shoulder. "I'll see you in Neverland, and we'll finish this conversation there. You're safe with me. For now, at least." Strong arms hefted me up as the icy claws of unconsciousness pulled me down into blissful nothingness.

Dampness touched my cheek, which forced my eyelids to pry apart. I was lying on the mossy ground of the meadow and birds were singing above me. Moaning at the irony of waking up with birds above my head like a *Looney Tunes* character who'd been KO'ed, I attempted to sit up.

All I had to say about it was, I'd better return home to seven small men cleaning the cottage with animals assisting them. Beneath me, flowers covered the ground, providing a soft mattress for my aching bones. To my left, I found the naked back of the antithesis of a storybook prince. Rowan's head turned, as if he'd heard me moving.

"You had an exciting day, darling," he said with a devilish smile playing on his sinful lips. Rising from a crouching position, he turned and edged toward me with slow, easy steps. "I take it the awakening Violet planned for you didn't go as planned?"

"If you mean my untimely demise, then no. I didn't stick around to let Grams murder me." Pulling my knees against my chest, I wrapped my arms around them.

"Your grandmother didn't intend to sacrifice you," he murmured as he knelt in front of me. "Violet is a lot of things, most of which I find abhorrent, but I'd bet she's an exemplary grandmother. Her intentions are good, but her execution needs some work."

"Nope, I think her execution was spot-on if her goal was

terror. There were men and women dancing naked around a bonfire. They were chanting and then their heads did the whole exorcist spiel, spun around and released black clouds of smoke from their throats. I'm smart enough to know that, when there's an altar involved, a bitch should already be running. So, I ran as fast as my feet would carry me. And then you . . . saved me?" While that seemed on brand for him since he'd saved me the night we'd met, something about that statement didn't feel accurate. Had their heads spun? Nope, but I was allowed to be dramatic after what I'd witnessed. It was probably the only thing they hadn't done, and it might have happened that way if I'd stuck around any longer. "How did you save me? Wait, am I dead?" I asked, noting the lack of excruciating pain in my feet.

"I wouldn't let you escape me by dying, Moira Darling. It wouldn't be very 'Peter Pan' of me, would it?"

I laughed humorlessly. "You're not Peter Pan. You're more of a Captain Hook, Rowan. I wouldn't place you in the category of 'hero'."

"Good, because I assure you, I'm not. Villains are much more fun to be with, anyway. Heroes end up playing to the rules of the world, and what would be the fun in that? Damsels need a hero because they think it will make them a princess at the end of the tale, but you? You don't strike me as someone who'd want to be a princess—not when you could be something far more important in your own tale. You'd prefer to be a witch in a world overpopulated with a princess in need of saving. Then you'd also need a villain willing to sacrifice everything and everyone to ensure you reached your full potential." He paused before adding, "Unless I'm wrong about you, but I'm hardly ever wrong about anything."

"That was really smooth, Teivel," I whispered as a smile lifted my lips. "But I'm feeling more like Alice when she fell down the rabbit hole." His eyes sparkled with mirth as something ruffled behind his back, before leathery wings unfurled behind him. His skin slowly began swirling with inky tendrils, which pulsed an electrical current into my naked arms. Awesome, he had the same smoking problem the cultists had. Was anyone normal anymore?

"Well, Alice? I guess you're about to discover that Wonderland's real and that you're the Queen of Hearts. Are you ready to discover the truth about magick, learn where it began, and find out what part you'll play in the game of good versus evil? I'll warn of this—you and I are not on the same side. Though, I don't intend to allow the enemies of either of our bloodlines to get their hands on you either. In the wrong hands, you'd destroy us all."

The End, For Now

ABOUT THE AUTHOR

Amelia Hutchins is a WSJ and USA Today Bestselling Author of the Monsters, The Fae Chronicles, and Nine Realm Series. She's an admitted coffee addict who drinks magical potions of caffeine and turns them into magical worlds. She writes alpha-hole males and the alpha women who knock them on their arses, hard. Amelia doesn't write romance. She writes fast-paced books that go hard against traditional standards. Sometimes a story isn't about the romance; it's about rising to a challenge, breaking through them like wrecking balls, and shaking up entire worlds to discover who they really are. If you'd like to check out more of her work, or just hang out in an amazing tribe of people who enjoy rough men, and sharp women, join her at Author Amelia Hutchins Group on Facebook.

Printed in Great Britain
by Amazon